B P

SILKE

Lacey Dancer

ZEBRA BOOKS
KENSINGTON PUBLISHING CORP.

ZEBRA BOOKS are published by

Kensington Publishing Corp.
850 Third Avenue
New York, NY 10022

First Zebra Printing: May, 1996
10 9 8 7 6 5 4 3 2 1

Printed in the United States of America

Prologue

He watched her from across the room. The sounds of the party filled the space between them but nothing could blunt her vivid flame. Her fiery red tresses flared with every movement of the dance as she swayed, enticed, bewitched, and beguiled the poor fool who all but drooled over the armful of curves he did his best to caress with every parry and retreat of the song. A circle had formed around the pair. Her head tipped back, golden brown lashes shielding molten eyes. A provocative pose from a woman who was probably born knowing how to intrigue, to captivate the unwary male animal. But he wasn't unwary, hadn't been since the first time he had tasted the fruit of passion. Like the woman she showed herself to be, he knew the sting of desire, understood the demanding drive. But unlike her, he controlled his needs, channeled them into productive courses, not self-destructive ones.

He lifted his drink to his lips, his gaze following her every move. But God, she was exquisite. She was reputed to have the morals of an alley cat but she was so beautiful it hurt to watch her—a hurt that reached past his libido to his soul. Surprising. Inconvenient. Impossible. He knocked back his drink, mentally cursing Silke Brown-St. James even as his body saluted her raw appeal.

Silke turned from the stranger with the black hair and the cold blue eyes, oddly unsettled by the way his gaze followed her every move. She, who rarely noticed those who coveted her body, found that she could remember every change of expression in his frozen lake eyes, the faint twist of his lips that said he didn't like what he saw but he was damn well going to watch her perform. A shiver traced her spine, angering her, bringing alive her temper. A dangerous combination when she was already high on adrenaline from the thin edge she walked. She tossed her head, her eyes glittering with fury barely leashed as she sent him one sizzling glance. Condemn her, would he? she challenged silently, throwing even more seduction into her dance. She hardly felt Ricky's arms tighten around her or noticed his faint frown of concern as he guided them to the doors that opened onto the terrace. The night air was cool on her skin, but nothing could dispel or touch the inner fire that drove her. The shadows of the gardens gathered around her, darkness to her vivid light. The man was a stranger to her and yet even now he held more of her attention than her escort, more of her attention than was even safe.

"You are definitely in rare form tonight," Ricky muttered, glaring at Silke even as he cradled her like a lover in his arms.

Silke shifted a languid shoulder, the excitement of the evening and the challenge of the silent man not even close to wearing off. It was even cooler here in this secluded corner, with shadows to hide the unsafe, a moon to caress lovers, a scent of flowers to whisper romance. And danger. Always danger in this land of the beautiful people, the wealthy children of those who had made money their god. She walked these halls and rooms, one of them but not one of them. She never forgot her real beginning. Her past was written in pain and suffering, her own and others. And now she paid the bills that she had been too young to address back then. She paid in the coin of risk, deception, and lies for a good cause. She paid in a ruined reputation, willfully destroyed to make her acceptable to this group that called her friend. She paid in the nightmares that no longer allowed for sleep until after dawn broke each day. She paid, not enough sometimes, too much others. Tonight it was a little of both.

"That's what I do best," she drawled finally. Ricky was her contact in this shadow world, the link between her and a man called Hollander whom she had never seen. These stolen moments, so intimate to any onlooker, were the minutes of information exchange so that no contact had to be made between her and the law enforcement community. Hollander had insisted on this cover, for her safety—what little there was—and the safety of those, like Ricky, who trod this path with her.

Ricky looked her over, silently if no other way, admitting she was right. No one ever suspected Silke Brown-St. James of having a brain, a focus, right or wrong. She was a party girl, fluff between her ears, flashy, sexy in clothes that were meant to raise a man's blood pressure. She oozed sensual appeal. "Do you know that guy who was watching you tonight?" He bent his head close to her neck, whispering the words against her skin. She smelled like heaven and woman. But because he loved the wife he left each night, he knew only the sharpness of the mind encased in the glorious body he held. Her scent was no more than window dressing, and her feel was necessary for the role both played with skill and courage.

Silke smiled faintly, giving him a smoldering look, her part of another game. She played so well sometimes that she had trouble deciding which was the real her. Or did Silke Brown even exist anymore? The question was a piece of the night and the horrors that robbed her of sleep. Habit and a will strengthened in a tough school slammed the lid on the thought that could only hurt and distract. She looked into Ricky's eyes, his lover to all who would watch them. "Which one? The one who tried to make a meal out of me on the dance floor before you cut in or the one with the midnight hair and the winter lake eyes who held up the northeast corner of the room?" She stroked his cheek, her nails vivid against the tan of his skin. He was safe. She knew about his wife, knew that no matter how much she played the seductress with this man that the actions would mean nothing, that he wouldn't take advantage of the role to take that which she would not give.

He laughed huskily. Her self-directed humor was always a surprise. "The guy with the black hair and blue eyes," he replied bluntly.

The image of the man was sharp, clear, demanding, and getting, even now, with the width of the night and the terrace, a response that had nothing to do with the job at hand. She knew better than to show Ricky that she remembered this one male more than the others. Although she felt she had earned a measure of Ricky's respect, she knew it would take little to have him question her commitment. His world was founded on distrust, a feeling that kept him alive.

"I have no idea. He isn't one of the crowd. Shall I ask around?" she replied offhandedly, her voice calculated to the last ounce of indifference.

"Hell, no!" Ricky exploded before he thought.

Silke's brows rose at the uncharacteristic vehemence. She searched his face, seeing an uneasiness that hadn't been there before. Her senses went on alert, the stranger sliding into the corners of her mind to be handled at another, safer time. "You sounded worried on the phone when you called me earlier. You asked for this meeting. Is something wrong?" The husky whispers were back, so soft that they didn't carry on the breeze.

Ricky bent his head again, his lips caressing her neck. "A lot is wrong. And it all is pointed in your direction. It seems our quarry is a lot smarter than the usual dealer. He's especially good in math and asking questions."

Although the languid movements that epitomized Silke's actions remained, a new tension invaded her body. Her lashes lifted from the normal sultry angle to reveal a golden gaze that held shrewdness rather than a sensual promise of bedroom delight. "Adding two and two, is he?"

Ricky didn't alter his position. Hollander had been very specific in his requirements, whatever it took. "Right. That's always been a risk. You knew that going in. We've been damn lucky to get this close to the top."

Silke read between the lines too well to be put off by a compliment. "Get to the point, Ricky."

"Hollander wants you out, ASAP. He wants the head man but not at the expense of a dead body."

"Especially one marked St. James," Silke finished for him, cradling his head to her.

"You said it. I didn't." Ricky looked away, then back at her, for once his eyes holding something more than professional interest in the amateur who had stumbled onto his home turf. "Tonight is the last night. He wants you out and he means out. In fact, if you can manage it, he wants you out of town."

"Or?"

Ricky covered his grimace with a kiss. "Or. He'll find a way to put you out."

"And we both know that won't be hard with what I have done to my reputation. Even my own family won't believe me innocent of anything with the possible exception of murder." Silke stared past him, thinking deeply. She had had a long run. The first few years had been so spotty that no one, not even Hollander, had believed

the information she had garnered had been anything more than
flukes. But these last four years had taken concentrated effort and
were very rewarding. They were very close to the top man. They
had his name and were even now preparing to tighten the net of the
legal system around his neck. But everything had to be letter perfect
for the case to stick. So everyone, Silke included, had walked the
thin line collecting every shred of evidence, every nail for this particular Dracula's coffin. There would be no night rising from the
dead for this dealer, no convenient loophole, no violation of rights,
no questionable arrest. Letter perfect was the way Hollander had
decreed the bust would go down, and so it would. Silke focused on
Ricky's concerned face, reading his need for her agreement. She
would give it, but not for him or even for herself. Rather for those
too far gone, too weak, or too young to fight for themselves.

"It looks like he leaves me with no other choice. To stay in is
to risk others besides myself. If that weren't the case, I'd tell him
to go to the devil," she replied flatly, giving Ricky only part of
the truth, the portion he would understand and accept without
question. Another role played to the audience. Another veil to
conceal or to strangle?

Ricky inclined his head, believing every clipped word. Silke
wasn't a woman given to idle promises or threats. She had guts,
more than most men and a lot more than any other woman he knew.
In his opinion that was her greatest strength and her worst weakness.
"I'll tell him." He hesitated, his hand coming up to stroke her cheek.
For the first time in their association the gesture was personal. "Can
I also tell him that you will be taking a long trip?"

Silke felt the difference immediately. The personal concern in
his eyes surprised her as much as the worry in his voice. Only
the fact that she could feel his worry as a friend kept her from
drawing away from this most innocent contact. To play the game
was acceptable. To make it real was impossible. Ever.

"I'll think about it," she answered quietly, finally. She smiled a
faint, natural smile that didn't match the femme fatale image for an
instant. Then she glanced over her shoulder to the doors spilling
golden light that didn't touch the shadows in which she and Ricky
stood. For one moment, she let the mask she donned almost every
night fall away. For one second, weariness all the way to her soul
held her thoughts. Then she shrugged, her body going fluid with the

return of the role she had chosen to play. Her lashes dropped, her mouth pouted as she raked icy fingers through her hair. She looked back at Ricky, swayed closer, offering him a taste of the pout, the lips whose red would smear just enough to excuse the time spent away from the party. "Make it good. We're very close to closing curtain," she whispered, just before she kissed him.

He watched her give her mouth to the slender man, his fingers clenching on the glass he held as the man's hands caressed the silken shoulders bared by that impossibly cut dress of iridescent green. He shouldn't have come tonight. It wasn't part of his job to let his quarry see his face but he hadn't been able to resist. A fool's move, but then this woman seemed to specialize in making fools of men. The poor sucker she held so intimately didn't seem to care that this woman had made a name for herself in picking up and discarding men. He didn't seem to notice that she was giving her mouth to him with no real feeling behind the kiss, that her hands touched him without desire, only its counterfeit facsimile. All Ricky seemed to see was the silk and velvet package, not the shallow heart and soul it covered. He tossed back his drink and set the glass on the ledge bordering the terrace, feeling the evidence of his own intense interest. He had never shared. He believed in discretion, commitment for as long as the loving lasted. Silke had no such rules. She had played to the men in the room beyond the darkness, her eyes flashing with feminine challenge to any and all. Then she had held each who had taken up that dare at arm's length mentally, emotionally. He hadn't believed it at first, certain that someone would touch her, bring some real emotion to those molten golden eyes. But no one had, not even the man with whom she was reputed to be sleeping. Disgusted with himself for caring what she was beyond the confines of the job he had to do, he turned his back on Silke Brown-St. James and all she represented. He would do his job. He was paid well, and his honor demanded full value for the money he received. But this was the first and last impulse where this red-haired, honey-eyed bewitcher was concerned.

One

The sun filled the gracious room, the sounds of the city locked away behind the black grilled gates with the St. James crest that guarded the estate. Rolling green Pennsylvania hills were dotted with decades-old shade trees. A lake on which regal swans glided with their young in springtime gave a parklike atmosphere to the grounds and winding paths that offered beautiful, serene views of the surrounding land. But despite the visual delight of the setting, the real jewel was the house. It predated the Civil War, had withstood that terrible time and the changes of fortune of the 1929 crash and all the human pain and tragedy that had followed the St. Jameses down through their history. The present owners were Lorraine Dayton-St. James and her husband Geoffrey. Both were in their late sixties, well known for their philanthropic work and charisma. One of their pet charities, founded by Lorraine Dayton-St. James some forty-five years before, was the Dayton-St. James Children's Facility situated across town.

The facility had given both Lorraine and her husband a measure of peace, of fulfillment for those barren years that had followed the realization that there would never be any children to continue the last of their respective genetic lines. Unlike many of their contemporaries, they found that consideration had been the second concern rather than the first. For in their era of arranged marriages between affluent families, theirs had been a match of love and a need to see an expression of that love in the form of children. But in spite of her moneyed and pampered background Lorraine was a practical woman. The medical field had yet to come up with a solution for her particular problem, so she, with Geoffrey's help, had solved it herself. First, she had established the facility and then, later, taken to her home and heart four young girls, each very different, coming from diverse and tragic backgrounds and desperately needing more than the average parents could provide. She and Geoffrey had loved their daughters of the heart, guided their footsteps toward maturity, suffered the pain of watching their mistakes, enjoyed and shared their triumphs, and waited. Waited for each of their chosen ones to find a mate, to fulfill her true potential. But they waited in vain. Geoffrey counseled patience. Lorraine reminded her spouse that C. R. and Silke, the two eldest daughters, were close to thirty and *something* had to be done. It had taken a month of planning, of discussion, of soul-searching but Lorraine had formulated *The Plan*. Today she would implement it.

"My dear, are you sure you still wish to go through with this?" Geoffrey asked worriedly. The sunlight pouring through the windows into their private breakfast room was kind, highlighting the aristocratic features with a gentle hand. But no matter how gentle the hand of nature, only a fool would mistake the strength and power of this aging boardroom warrior. "We're asking a lot of them. To give up a year of their lives, move to another city, start over. Even though we have minimized the danger by hiring Killian's company to provide bodyguards for each of them, your plan still contains elements of risk. I know you, my dear. If something goes wrong, you will blame yourself. I won't have you hurt."

Lorraine didn't dispute his truth. They knew and understood each other too well for lies to ever be possible between them. "I wish we could have thought of another way but we didn't. I know my plan is drastic and risky. But we just can't stand by and watch all of them throw their lives away. Silke's reputation is in shreds. The gossips never let her alone. The newspapers make a fortune on each installment of Silke St. James. C. R. is becoming more aggressive, denying her gender with every hour. She dresses as though she despises her own sex. She is so driven. Leora has the strength of a wet paper towel, always shrinking away from others, from herself. And Noelle acts as though she doesn't know there is a reality. And not one of them, when I spoke to them privately last month, thinks there is anything wrong with her choices or her life. We have tried to give them every material advantage and a loving, stable environment. But maybe those very things have deprived them of the challenge of living. With their histories, maybe they need that challenge to thrust them out of themselves into the real world." She searched his eyes, needing his strength, knowing it would be there for her. "I can't bear to think that our interference with their lives could have denied them the path to their full potential."

He took her hand, holding it tightly, his worry for her and their daughters clear in his eyes. "You are pinning so much hope on this idea. What if they don't agree? Will you be able to walk away from this, watch from the sidelines?"

"I don't know," she admitted with a sigh. "I am praying as I haven't in years. We've tried everything else. The best counselors for Leora and Noelle right after we brought them here. The same for Silke and C. R., although neither of them did more than stonewall the therapists with silence and closed minds. We've educated them, loved them, but we haven't given them freedom from us and our influence. I feel like I'm cutting out my heart to ask this of them but I can't not do it. I believe in them, their strengths, their courage, and their ingenuity. They just need a push to come to terms with their pasts, present, and futures."

Geoffrey carried her hand to his lips, watching her as he kissed her fingers. "Then it will work, my love. Somehow, it will work. Like you, I believe in them." A knock at the outer door drew his eyes. "That will be Grimes to tell us our chicks have arrived." He stood, her hand still in his. "Shall we get this campaign started?"

Lorraine squeezed his fingers once more, then rose gracefully to her feet. She was a reed-slim woman, unbowed by age. Her eyes were a gentle hazel, her hair delicately blond and cut in a bell to shape the contours of her face. She looked soft, very feminine, but steel lurked beneath the silk and pearls. Lorraine was one of those women who could do more with the lift of a slender, elegantly arched brow than another could do with an oath and a pocket full of temper.

"Do you come with me?"

He shook his head. "No. I think I'll entertain Killian and his men until you get to them."

She laughed softly. "What you mean is, you'll convince him that I haven't lost my mind with this idea."

His eyes twinkled at her. "My pet, no man of your or my

acquaintance would ever be that foolish. You might choose unusual ways of achieving your ends, but achieve them you do."

They walked together out of the study, nodding to Grimes, the
butler. They separated in the main hall, each to do a share of the
delicate task they had set for love of their children.

"I wonder what Mother wants," Noelle murmured vaguely. She
was a slender woman, all violet eyes, straight black hair to her
waist, and long limbs. She was delicately formed, giving the im-
pression that a whisper of sound would damage her fragile balance. Yet for all the gifts that nature had chosen to bestow on her,
Noelle never looked quite put together. There was always something a bit untidy about her, a thread hanging, a smear of eye
shadow where it shouldn't be. Even today, the hyacinth dress that
just skimmed her curves with the row of buttons from neckline
to hem had two buttons missing near the bottom. Her hair was
mussed ever so slightly.

Silke noticed Noelle's appearance but made no comment as she
leaned back in her chair, nursing her cigarette. Like the rest of
the family, she had given up on Noelle's strange habits. She
glanced at the door to her mother's sitting room, wishing for the
hundredth time that Lorraine had called this meeting at a reasonable hour. After a night like last night, the only thing that had
any value was a bed and six hours, or four in a pinch, of unin-
terrupted sleep. She took another drag on the cigarette, silently
damning the habit that she used only in situations where she
needed to stay on her toes and look as though she weren't. She
crossed her nylon-clad legs, the narrow white heels she wore adding inches to her five-foot-four frame. The white dress that
matched the heels was simplicity itself, but on her body it had a
sensuality that couldn't be missed. And unlike Noelle, every hair
and button was in place, her makeup superb despite the speed
with which she had prepared for this meeting.

"Whatever it is, I hope it's more important than my meeting
with Martelle. There is a lot riding on this contract," C. R. replied,
glancing at her narrow-banded, utilitarian watch. A faint line of
irritation lay between her brows, but other than that no other sign
of distress showed. She wore her usual gray suit, tailored, trim,

and conservative. Only small studs in her ears softened the effect of the boardroom costume.

Before the fourth member of the family could speak, the door to their mother's private sitting room was opened by Grimes and Lorraine glided into view.

"Good morning, my dears," Lorraine said as she took a chair behind the desk from which she conducted her not inconsiderable charity work. She folded her hands and surveyed her daughters. Each was unique. Silke with her improbable name that exactly matched the texture of her ivory skin. That flaming hair was an indication of her temper and the golden eyes a hint to the gentleness that she showed only those few who commanded her love. Of all her children, Silke was the most difficult to understand, to get close to. Lorraine liked to believe that she had succeeded in the latter, but she knew, in part, that she was only fooling herself. No matter how much Silke loved her adoptive parents, there remained a core of secrecy, of aloofness about her. Even her history was shrouded in mystery, and only Silke held the key.

"Mother, could we please know why you wished to see us all together?" C. R. asked in her role, long ago assigned, as spokesperson for the quartet.

Lorraine inclined her head as she turned to Caprice. Mentally, she grimaced at the outfit Caprice had chosen. She could still remember the vivid colors that Caprice had favored when she had first come to them. Like Silke, she had a temper, but it was rarely seen these days. Lorraine sighed deeply as she pushed the memories aside. "As you wish." She lifted four thick envelopes, sealed and bearing each of their names. "As you know, next year I will be seventy. Contrary to custom, I have chosen my own gift. I would like each of you to give me a year out of your lives." As she spoke, she watched each face, gauging each reaction.

The announcement had the effect of doing what nature and the hand of the legal system had never been able to do. Lorraine's four daughters suddenly had something in common beyond the love of their adoptive parents. They all wore identical expressions of shock and bewilderment.

Silke's mind raced behind the screen of emotion. Lorraine was capable of almost anything to get her way if she felt she was just in her decision. Silke had been treated to an extended critique of her personal life a little over a month ago. She had come away from the interview knowing her adoptive mother was disturbed, but Silke was bound by promises and risks to lives other than her own to hold her tongue. She had waited for Lorraine to push for a change, known she would do her best to satisfy this woman who had offered her so much more than the material advantages of being one of the St. James family of Pennsylvania. But the push had never come, and in the demands of the life she led, both real and shadowed, she had tucked the interview away.

"To do what?" Silke asked when it appeared no one else would speak.

Lorraine smiled, as always reacting to the challenge of pitting herself against another mind or, in this case, four minds. "To right your father's and my wrongs."

Silke frowned, confusion displacing shock. "What wrongs?"

"Well, my dear, our parenting obviously isn't very good or we wouldn't have four beautiful young women who, in their own special ways, are each determined to ignore any possibility of a meaningful relationship, the creating of a personal life with some value, and the giving of themselves to something other than just day-to-day survival."

"But Mother," Leora, the shy one of the group and always the last to assert herself, was moved to protest. For once her stammer was absent.

Lorraine turned her fine eyes on her youngest, waiting patiently. A wasted effort, for the minute attention was focused on Leora, she lost whatever words she might have spoken. Lorraine sighed and dropped the envelopes back on the desk.

"I had hoped by speaking to all of you individually last month that I would make some difference in the paths that each of you has chosen. C. R. is determined to race up the ladder of success to the exclusion of all else. Leora is working at being as invisible as possible. Noelle spends her days wandering around in the clouds so completely it's a wonder she hasn't walked off the end of the earth, and you, Silke, apparently are intending to go for some sort of record in engagements. What is the current score? Five or six in the last three years?" The sarcasm was loaded into the soft, full tones of each word.

All four women straightened in their chairs. Lorraine's temper was rarely felt, and never had any of them known the sting of her articulate tongue.

"So, I'm taking matters into my own hands. Now, of course, you're at liberty to refuse my challenge, but I'm praying that for your sakes you won't." She rose, picked up the envelopes, and gave one to each woman. "Inside, you will find a plane ticket to a different destination, a set of keys to a middle-class used car, and three thousand in cash. The day after tomorrow, if you agree, I will expect you to give to me all your credit cards, keys to your apartments and cars, and every cent of cash you have in your possession beyond the three thousand. In addition, you will take with you only two suitcases, packed with any clothes and personal hygiene products you need, but nothing else. You will then board your respective planes, collect your cars at the destinations, and set out to learn just what you are as individuals without the St. James name and money to cushion your way. You will find some way of earning a living, rent a place to do that living, and make friends on your own, of your own."

Lorraine leaned her hip against the desk and watched the changes of expressions in her audience. "I'm asking a lot of all four of you, each in different ways. But if I didn't believe in this course, if you hadn't left me with no other alternatives, I wouldn't have needed this kind of drastic action. Geoffrey agrees with me on this. Our whole intent when we chose each of you to become part of our family was to offer you a complete life and a chance for a whole future. It was never our intent for you to use the material advantages we were able to provide as shields, barriers, and bunkers. We love you too much to continue to let this happen without trying to change it. So I'm asking, no, we're both begging, that each of you will look at your life this morning, understand what we see, or at least try to understand and to give us and yourselves this year."

"And if nothing changes?" C. R. demanded, the logistics of what Lorraine was asking too demanding to consider. Her whole life was going up in smoke on the basis of a whim. Every instinct demanded she fight back. The love she had for the woman standing in front of her was the only barrier to outright refusal. She didn't look at her sisters, certain they felt as she did.

Lorraine sighed deeply, suddenly appearing older than her

years. "Then Geoffrey and I will say nothing more about your life-styles."

"We won't have a life to come back to," C. R. replied bitterly. "Or, at least I won't. I can't just walk away in the middle of a deal like the one I am putting together. You're asking me to give up everything I've worked for."

"I'm asking you to make a detour, not give up anything. All of you will have exactly what you have now or better when you return. Your father and I will keep your apartments going, your cars and bills in order, and in your case, Caprice, Geoffrey will hold your job for you. In short, both Geoffrey and I are determined none of you will lose anything with my plan but time."

C. R., Caprice, sighed angrily, knowing she couldn't put forth any more material objections. Lorraine had neatly blocked that course.

Silke stared down at the package in her hand. Her mother's plan was bizarre to say the least, but very like Lorraine when she believed in a cause. She looked up, studying each of her sisters in turn. Her mother had been right on target with each of her assessments. They, herself included, were using the St. James name and money to cushion their weaknesses, even the so perfect C. R. As for herself, she wouldn't really be missed by anyone but Geoffrey, Lorraine, and her sisters. She, of the four of them, had the least to lose and the most to gain. Ricky would breathe a sigh of relief and Hollander would sleep at nights even if she couldn't.

"I'll go," she said slowly, distinctly, watching Lorraine's reaction. The faint flicker of surprise touched her temper even though she knew she deserved the reaction.

Lorraine held her look for a second before Noelle's wispy voice interrupted.

"Me too." She glanced at Leora.

Leora's fingers shook as she twisted her envelope in her hands. "I'll . . . go," she stammered.

Everyone looked at C. R. She held out for a moment, her fingers restlessly tracing the sharp edges of the envelope. "All right. I'll be damned if I'll be the only one to hold out. But I want to go on record saying this is a crazy idea. As far as I'm concerned I think my priorities are fine. I know what I want and where I'm going."

Lorraine didn't bother to respond to the challenge. She had said her words. It was time for action. "Open your envelopes, my dears, and we will go over the specifics."

Killian Carpenter hooked one ankle over a knee and tried to relax when he felt like doing anything else. He'd rather be in the dentist office—he hated that with a passion—than facing Lorraine and Geoffrey St. James and listening to this crazy scheme that Lorraine had hatched. But a job was a job. His company specialized in the unusual, and his men were highly trained investigators and watchdogs for the elite. Normally, he wouldn't have been considering a field assignment. His days of that wearying existence were long since over. But an epidemic of summer flu had left him shorthanded and the St. Jameses were clients as well as friends. So here he was, babysitter glorified for a young woman with more money than sense, more looks than discretion, and more temper than restraint. Silke Brown-St. James was not the assignment of the man whose place he was taking. But as far as he was concerned, she represented the greatest challenge to the person sent to watch discreetly over her, protect, and if necessary befriend her as she made her way in the real world. Lorraine's plan might have been crazy in his opinion, but Geoffrey and she had done their best to make sure that their daughters didn't go undefended into reality. Beside him sat three of his best operatives who would act as guards for the other daughters.

"Are you really worried about this plan?" Geoffrey asked as he passed Killian the last cup of coffee he poured. He leaned back against the cushions of the couch and studied the man he respected and liked as he did few others.

"If you are asking if I am worried about the girls' safety, then no." Killian sipped carefully, his gaze holding the older man's over the rim of the cup. "They'll be as safe as here, probably safer, with one of us watching their backs every minute."

"But?"

Killian sighed. Geoffrey was astute and believed in asking impossible questions and receiving very possible answers. "I just think the whole thing is a last-ditch attempt. It isn't as if any of them will ever really have to work for a living. They will be taking a year's vacation with a little work thrown in. In short, they'll be playing at living. I don't see how that's going to make any kind of effective change in their mind-sets."

"So you think it is acceptable for them to be nothing more than polite parasites?" Lorraine commented, coming in just in time to hear his reply.

Killian turned his head, his gaze steady, direct. "A lot of their contemporaries are doing the same thing, and no one is worried about them or coming up with a complete break from the family for a year for the erring offspring to get it together."

Lorraine laughed softly, undisturbed by the sting in his remarks. "You sound like C. R."

Killian controlled a grimace. Corporate sharks of the female kind had never appealed.

"You don't like that." Lorraine sat down on the sofa next to her husband. "Which one are you watching?"

"Silke."

Lorraine nodded, unsurprised by the choice and privately pleased. Of the four, Silke probably had the greatest potential for trouble, and Killian, despite his retirement from active field work, was the best of his company—at least that was Geoffrey's opinion.

"Did they all agree?" Killian asked, getting to the point of the meeting. He had a lot to do this morning if he was to be gone from the office for an indefinite time. Fortunately, Silke had a track record for not finishing anything, so the chance of his having to stay the full year as her shadow was remote. Not that he couldn't hand her off when his staff was back to full force, but unlike Silke, he always finished what he started.

Lorraine laughed softly, genuine amusement glittering in her eyes. "Oddly enough, Silke was the first. She surprised me. I thought either she or C. R. would be the last. I think this morning's hangover is the full reason."

Mentally swearing a few choice oaths, Killian did his best to keep his mind off the sexy redhead who was responsible for his loss of sleep last night. That damn party she had attended hadn't been worth the name, not that she had seemed to care. She had danced with anyone who asked, had always had a drink in her hand, and had been the center of attention in spite of the other beauties who had been there. In short, she had been the flash of the evening, sheer glitz with no heart. Just the kind of woman a man bedded without respecting. Of the four, Silke was the reason that Killian had any sympathy at all for Lorraine's mad plan.

"I'll take care of your daughter." He glanced at his employees, holding each pair of steady eyes for a second before moving on. "We all will."

Two

Silke yawned and stretched, her nude body shifting gracefully on the pink silk sheets. The late afternoon sun was filtered out of the room by satin drapes of a deeper shade. The carpet was pristine white, the furniture sleek and ash oak. It was a beautiful room, rich, appealing to the senses, but a room that hardly seemed the perfect choice for a natural redhead. But Silke did nothing expected. Pink was her favorite color, so carrot hair be damned. Pink she would have.

Slipping out of the bed, she strolled to the en suite bath with its rose marble tile and gold fittings. An hour of soaking in her own special blend of spicy scent chased away the last of the fatigue from the night before. Not bothering with anything more than a cream silk robe, she wandered toward the kitchen for something to put into her empty stomach. While she was deciding, she punched the play button on her answering machine. The worried voices of each of her younger sisters were interesting contrasts to C. R.'s brisk, no-nonsense tones. Yet, the pair of them had left only one message each asking her to call. Caprice—Silke was the only one besides their mother who dared call C. R. by her real name—had left three messages, the last a statement of intent to arrive at five. Silke glanced at the clock and grimaced. Her food would have to wait. The best she could hope for was a glass of her special fresh-squeezed orange juice concoction. Working quickly, competently, she made a pitcher while the glass was chilling. She had barely finished cleaning up when security called to inform her C. R. had arrived.

Silke met her at the door, receiving a glare for her lack of dress. "I just got up," she murmured mildly, gesturing Caprice into the apartment.

"One time in my life I'd like to see you get your days and nights straight like a normal person," Caprice muttered, tossing her jacket over the chair on which she had dropped her briefcase. She kicked off her shoes and swore once.

Silke clicked her tongue as she watched the uncharacteristic display. "You are in a state, Caprice." She grinned when Caprice shot her a lethal glare. "You've had most of the day to come to terms with our mother's idea and you still look like you're going to explode."

Caprice didn't dispute the last for the simple reason it was very close to the truth of the way she felt after having had to scramble around for the last eight hours and reassign her work to others. "If you love me, don't call me that." Caprice released the pins from her sensible hairstyle and shook out the heavy mass of white blond.

"What you do to your hair is a crime. You ought to be shot."

Caprice ignored the provocation that she had heard in varying forms for as long as she could remember. "The one who ought to be shot is Mother," she said instead. "And Father, of course, for going along with this mess." Caprice flung herself down on the couch and eyed Silke's slender length with disfavor. "I'm surprised you agreed so quickly or at all. The last I heard you were going at it hot and heavy with some guy named Ricky."

"I didn't know you kept up with my love life." Silke curled sinuously into the cushions on the other end of the couch. "Would you like a drink?" she asked as an afterthought. She waved her half-full glass invitingly.

C. R.'s glare intensified. "Will you stay sober long enough to make sense?"

"It's after five," Silke murmured, not bothering to correct C. R.'s interpretation of her drinking habits. Actually, she hated the taste of liquor and rarely drank more than wine with her meals. But the crowd she ran with expected a certain code of behavior, and since she did not do drugs, she had to appear to do something.

C. R. groaned and dropped her head in her hands, instantly contrite. Of all of her sisters, for some odd reason, Silke was the one she came to when she needed to blow off steam. "I'm sorry.

I shouldn't have said that. You don't pass judgment on me. I have no right to criticize your life."

Silke laughed, the sound beguiling even to another woman. It invited the listener to partake of life, savor the bitter and the sweet, and come back for more. "Don't worry about it. I've got a thick skin." She rose with languid grace and strolled to the bar to pour Caprice the same as she was having. "Try it. I promise it won't turn you into a Silke clone." Her eyes glittered pure devil's gold.

Caprice took the glass, a seldom seen grin tilting the edges of her mouth. She took a taste, then another larger one. "This is good. What's in it?"

"A little of this and a little of that." Silke sat down again and curled her legs under her. "To get back to our illustrious mother, I think she's right. None of us is much, you know." She patted Caprice's back as she choked on her orange juice. "Even you, my dear sister," she drawled before Caprice could get enough breath back to defend herself. "When was the last time you had a date? Went to a party? Had a day off? Did something just for the hell of it? Your life is as one-dimensional as it can get. As for Leora, she helps mother with the office work for her charities, but what else does she do? Nothing. She's so afraid of people that it hurts. And Noelle, beyond those truly marvelous paintings that she won't allow to be shown or sold, defends herself with enough vague behaviors and utterances to confound any man, woman, or child. As for me, I'm a lush, a party girl, not to be taken seriously and certainly not respected."

Caprice didn't believe in fighting losing battles, so she didn't take issue with the summations. "Mother knew what she was taking on when she chose us. Each one of us has a reason for the way we are, how we live." Memories, dark and hurtful, crowded Caprice's mind, unlocking the truth. "Of all of us, in some ways you have the best attitude. At least you go out and meet life. Leora, Noelle, and I are still hiding from it. I think I've envied you for being able to live for the moment."

Silke absorbed Caprice's honesty, feeling it all the way to her shadowed soul. For one second, she almost shared a part of herself that no one else knew. However, the risk was too great, not only to herself but to others. She had to stay in character, at least most of the way in character. "It's the only thing we have. The future is only a word, never a reality. Tomorrow never really comes. And yesterday only applies when you allow it that power."

Caprice stared at Silke. Of all her sisters, Silke was the most mysterious, while at the same time seeming to be an open book of well-read verses. But never had Caprice known her to attempt to be profound. "Did you get hurt, Silke? Did this creep do something? Is that why you want to leave?" With every question, Caprice's voice softened, becoming more caring.

Silke felt the sting of guilt for what she was about to do. "Something like that." She took a hefty swallow of her drink, then set it down. "But most of all, I need a change. Maybe it won't be a real change in the end, but like Mother says, at least it's a chance to try." She touched Caprice's hand. Oddly, despite her background, her lack of trust in most things human, she still reached out physically and emotionally to her family. "I truly do think this chance will be good for all of us. Maybe we won't change any of the physical attributes of our lives, but I'm betting the insides of us will change and that has to be for the better."

Caprice thought for a moment, searching for answers. "Maybe I do get lonely, but essentially I like the way I am," she protested, surprised to discover she could speak freely with Silke about things she had always kept hidden.

"Do you remember when you had a temper?"

Caprice frowned, startled at the years she hadn't thought of in a long time. "Yes. What does that have to do with anything?"

"Don't you think it odd that you never give in to that now?"

"Not odd. Smart. That temper put me in juvenile hall."

There were none so blind as those so certain they were right. For the first time in her life, Silke felt sorry for Caprice. "It also brought you to St. James's and then to Lorraine and Geoffrey.

Caprice couldn't deny that truth. "Get to the point."

"The point is that none of us can deny where we came from. Not Leora with her abusive background. Or Noelle with her abandonment to the streets. Not you with three broken homes behind you and no name for your father."

"Or you with the mother who earned money for her drug habit from men without names."

Silke didn't flinch from the reality of her past. She knew it too intimately to fear it. "We all try in our own ways. We wear beautiful clothes, go to all the right places, have degrees behind our names, and know which fork to use, but inside, not one of us, if we are honest, sees herself for what she is, only what she was. The unwanted, the victim, the unloved, the used, the abused. I, for one, want to crack that mirror. I'm tired of remembering."

Caprice stared at Silke, stunned at the depth she could have sworn didn't exist in her live-for-today sister. "I thought I was the only one of us who couldn't forget," she confessed finally, feeling each word being drawn out of a festering wound. "I've damned myself every morning that I wake up and look around counting furniture and clothes, reminding myself that I haven't been moved in the middle of the night to escape the bill collectors or to leave one more father behind. I didn't let myself think about Noelle and Leora either. I just accepted that the way they were was the way they would always be." She was ashamed of her blindness, ashamed that Silke with her partying ways had seen more than she. "I owe you an apology."

Silke shook her head, seeing the guilt in Caprice's eyes. "No you don't. I painted you and everyone else a picture of myself. I can't cry or condemn because you believed it."

Caprice looked down at the glass she still held, studying it rather than those beautiful eyes that seemed to see her better than she saw herself. "This doesn't have anything alcoholic in it, does it?" she asked, suddenly realizing that despite the large amount she had drunk, there was no alcoholic effect.

Silke rose, turning her back for an instant on Caprice's need. She wasn't ready for any unmasking, but it appeared fate and her own mouth had decreed otherwise. "No. Only a little pineapple juice, peppermint flavoring, lemon-lime soda, and orange juice. And of course, a cherry." She turned, waiting for the next question.

Caprice studied her, wondering just what else she had missed through her own willful blindness. "The engagements?"

"Real enough."

"Who left whom? We've all believed it was you walking away out of boredom or a search for greener pastures."

Silke almost smiled. This honest she was not yet prepared to be. But she could part with a portion of the truth. "They did the walking."

"Why?"

"Now, that, my dear sister, I'm not ready to tell. I may never be."

Caprice wanted to argue, but the flash of agony in Silke's eyes stunned her enough to dam the words unspoken. "If you ever do need someone to listen, I'd be honored if you chose me," she said instead.

Silke studied her, as surprised by the offer as Caprice had been by her insight. "You mean that, don't you?" she murmured finally. "Do you know I don't believe I have ever thought about talking to anyone?"

"Me either." Caprice rose, padded barefoot to the bar in front of which Silke stood, and picked up a bottle of vodka. "I'm beginning to agree with Mother after all, much as it kills me to admit it." She unscrewed the lid and splashed a good amount of the clear liquid in her half-full glass.

Silke's brows rose at the uncharacteristic action. "What are you doing?"

Caprice gave her a grin that almost rivaled Silke's own for mischief. "I'm going for the first buzz in my life. And after that, you're going to take me to one of your parties." She looked down at herself, grimacing at her dull attire. "But in between those two, you'll have to loan me some clothes. I don't have a thing to wear of my own even if I was in the mood to go back to the apartment to change. Which I'm not." She slanted Silke a glance. "How do you feel about uninvited guests of the female variety? I don't snore or walk in my sleep. And I can be very discreet if necessary."

Silke laughed, for the first time seeing the sense of humor that Caprice had always kept under tight wraps since she reached her majority. "I can live with it for a night as long as it isn't a steady diet. But I don't have one party on for tonight."

Caprice's brows rose. "Not one?" she repeated blankly.

Silke laughed at her shock. "No. I wish you could see your face. You look as if I just stole your favorite client."

Caprice ignored the reference to business. She knew she would regret her intemperate behavior tomorrow, but she would worry about that then. "But I probably won't ever be this brave again." She knocked back a taste of the drink she had made and found it good enough for a second taste. "Or this pot valiant," she added as she felt the warmth reach her stomach.

Silke really laughed then. Caprice was so disappointed Silke was almost tempted to lead her sister down the red brick road for one night. If there hadn't been the danger of someone linking Caprice to her and the party scene that was growing more risky by the hour, Silke would have done it. "What if I cook you some dinner instead?"

"You can cook?" Caprice snagged the vodka before Silke could ease her past it.

"Actually, I can. Very well as a matter of fact."

"I can't cook." She obeyed Silke's push that seated her with a thump on the stool drawn up in front of the work island.

Silke topped off Caprice's glass with juice, hoping to dilute the vodka. Caprice's quick consumption of the excess, then her refill with more alcohol, ruined that strategy. "I'd go easy on that. You aren't used to it."

"I'm changing."

Silke shook her head before she turned to the refrigerator. "Just don't say I didn't warn you."

Killian studied the three men seated before him in his private study. He had handpicked each for his ability and personality. None had permanent ties in Philly. "You've each had plenty of time to go over the dossiers. Has anyone got any last-minute questions?"

He waited for three negative responses. "All right. The women will be leaving the day after tomorrow. I expect each of you to stay on your particular assignment's trail. Any personal contact you have with them is strictly on a platonic level. In short, don't get involved. If, at any time in the next twelve months, any of you feels in danger of losing your objectivity, I want to know immediately and I'll bring in a replacement. Your job is strictly guard duty. We don't want those women hurt. They are part of a well-known family and all of them will be using their real names. As for any personal relationships they may make, you will investigate each, male and female. As long as there is nothing criminal in the background, you will retain your watcher status. Beyond that, report any problems immediately and the family and I will decide how to proceed."

Again he waited for nods to confirm their understanding. "And finally, make certain that you keep an eye on your quarry at the destination point. That is the real risk factor when we don't know where they will be staying. I'm counting on you not to lose them. The tracer bugs we placed in their cars only have so much range. Make sure you don't exceed them."

"What if they run into trouble getting settled?" the operative assigned to Noelle asked. "Do we help?"

His contemporaries grinned. Killian gave him a sympathetic look. "Only as far as their safety is involved."

The man grimaced. "Then I will be holding mine's hand the whole time."

Killian shook his head. "You know that's not the point of this exercise."

Noelle's guardian started to open his mouth. Killian held up his hand. "Just do the best you can and remember what you're there for. I chose each of you because you're the most flexible of the group. I'm counting on you all to play the game by feel and make it work. The last thing I want is one of these women hurt."

"We'll take care of it, boss," C. R.'s man said as he got to his feet. The rest followed suit. "Anything else?"

Killian shook his head, then watched them leave. He hadn't really needed this last meeting any more than they had. He was filling time, uneasy with this job in a way that he rarely was. And he knew the cause. One Silke St. James. He had cautioned his men against becoming involved with their assignments, but he had already broken his own rule. By rights he should have found himself a replacement. But he wouldn't. For heaven or hell, he was in.

He swore once, anger and frustration finding little outlet in the short word as he pulled a pad toward him and picked up a pen. He still had a lot to do before he could leave. He worked steadily for an hour, stopping once to pour himself a cup of coffee. Finally, he finished and leaned back in his chair with a deep sigh. Nursing the last of the lukewarm drink, he surveyed the final instructions he had just printed out for his office staff. Until that crazy Silke settled in one place, he couldn't even give his office a number to call beyond his portable cellular phone. He picked up her picture, studying the sultry eyes that seemed to know more about the world of man than he knew existed. Even in a one-dimensional form the woman was lethal. She challenged as she stared up at him, dared him to take her, to hold her when no one else had succeeded in doing so. She was flame. But he was the one burning.

"Damn her," he muttered, dropping the picture. He didn't want to think about in whose arms she danced this night, in whose bed she slept. He didn't want to know how many men had tasted those lips, run their fingers through that fiery hair. He didn't want to remember the scent that was so uniquely her own that lingered in the air to taunt and tease the senses. "Double damn her," he added hoarsely, knowing he was lying to himself.

He rose, shrugged into the leather bomber jacket that hung from a hook at the back of the small closet in the study, and then left the house. He needed to drive, to work off some of his thoughts and settle his mind on the business at hand. He couldn't hope to watch Silke as he had been hired to do feeling this way. If he had been the kind of man who substituted one woman for another, he would have filled his bed just to calm his overactive libido. Instead he drove, letting the concentration and skill needed for night driving take his thoughts and guide his direction. Unfortunately, his guide was as traitorous as his desire. He ended up in front of Silke's apartment building. Her windows were lit, the drapes drawn. Once in a while he could see a silhouette move, one he identified easily. The other was taller, leaner, short-haired. He didn't even know his curses were long, to the point, and graphic.

"I think I ought to cut it, I tell you," Caprice insisted, staring at the tightly pinned hair in the vaguely masculine style she had managed in spite of her clumsy fingers.

Silke stood behind her, studying the effect. Caprice had taken it into her head to try to change her image, and nothing Silke had been able to do had altered her decision. Not that Silke didn't agree, but Caprice was in no condition right now to be making any clear decisions. "And I tell you, you look like a woman trying to be a man." She shook her head at the sleek style that was simply too stark to be truly attractive.

"You fix it then," Caprice challenged her, holding Silke's gaze in the mirror.

Silke sighed in resignation. "I never realized how stubborn you are," she muttered.

"You said yourself that I need a new look. A more sem . . . feminine look," she answered, stumbling over the word.

"What you really need is a gallon of black coffee." The hurt look on her sister's face killed the rest of her objections. "All right. If you're determined to do this tonight, I'll try. This stupid tie has got to go." Putting her hands on Caprice's shoulders, she turned her sister around and stripped the offending accessory from Caprice's neck, then flicked open three buttons of her Oxford-style blouse. Hands on Caprice's hips, she hiked up her skirt enough to display an elegant length of leg. They nearly bumped heads as Caprice tried to watch the transformation in progress.

Caprice stumbled, reeling away from the contact, losing her balance. Silke grabbed for her. One of the glass tables that dotted the living room was too close for safety. Off balance herself, Silke managed to swing around, pulling Caprice out of harm's way. In a half clinch, they fell as one into the chair beside them, Silke on the bottom, Caprice sprawled across her legs.

Silke blew the hair out of her eyes, panting a little. "You aren't light, my dear sister," she groaned, feeling a number of aches. "It's a good thing we don't have an audience or we'd both end up looking as though women were our choice of fare."

Caprice moaned, holding her head with one hand and trying to shift her weight enough with the other to get up. "Will you just push or something? I feel like a fool. Why the devil did you let me drink so damn much?"

Silke gave a good hefty heave, and Caprice half slithered, half stood, swaying. Silke rose and wrapped her arm around Caprice's waist. "Lean on me before you topple over again. This place isn't safe for falling down drunks."

"I am not falling down drunk," Caprice protested indignantly. The effect was spoiled as she stumbled over a nonexistent lump in the carpet.

Silke hid a smile as she guided Caprice into the guest room. She had no doubt that, in the morning, Caprice was going to be in one very irritated mood. Her sister hated being out of control. And tonight, she had been just that. "Don't worry about it, kid. It will be our secret anyway."

* * *

Killian's eyes narrowed on Silke's window. His hands clenched around the steering wheel. Whoever was with her had almost attacked her, the damn fool. Not that Silke was objecting. She had her arms around the creep, holding him as though she would never let him go.

"The least the pair of them could have done was perform their bedroom calisthenics farther from the window. Every Peeping Tom in town is getting a free show," he muttered as the last of the lights went out. He started his car to return to his own empty bed. "At least I've seen with my own eyes just what she is," he added bitterly. "This is going to be the longest few months of my life." But while his mind heard the words, his body was listening to a different song, a siren's song. And her name was Silke.

Three

Silke looked her image over for the final time. Her so-called friends were giving her a farewell party at the club tonight. Ricky was sure to have heard through the gold-plated network the news of her impending trip and its reason. Hollander was probably dancing a jig while Ricky said his prayers with a clear conscience. Neither man had wanted her involved in their efforts to nail the largest drug dealer in Eastern Pennsylvania. Only the fact that their ongoing investigation had netted only small, highly expendable fish since its inception five years earlier had convinced them to give her a chance. Now all that was over. The investigation would continue but she wouldn't be there to see its end. Not that the glory of the thing mattered to her, but she had invested a great deal in the outcome and, unknown to either Ricky or Hollander, she had a number of scores to settle. For one moment, her eyes darkened to hammered gold, a look on her face no one had ever seen. Shattered innocence, total knowledge of man and his cruelties lay in her eyes. Memories, pitch-dark agony to recall, to blight an existence that sometimes seemed more a dream than reality. Caprice had her demons; they all did. But Silke was glad her own had lodged in her mind rather than theirs. No one deserved her memories. But those memories were what drove her to risk everything for those like herself who still walked the path down which she had almost been forced, for those who survived, barely, and those who didn't make it at all. For those who got out. For those who came to believe in the end that they were worth nothing more than what others thought of them. Children, all of them. Innocents who had no one to protect and shelter them from the wolves with honeyed voices and illusions for promises.

She smiled cynically at her own reflection. She was a strange-looking avenger for the innocent, with her wild mane of red hair, unblemished white skin, and cat-yellow eyes. Her gown was brown velvet, designed as a bustier in the bodice with a slim skirt to the floor to finish. The detailing of the undergarment cut was in gold thread and lace. It was an extravagant creation, barbaric, demanding attention as all of her clothes did. Beaten gold earrings set with yellow diamonds, a chain around her neck, two bracelets on one arm, and sleek brown velvet heels completed the look.

"I might be leaving tomorrow afternoon but I won't go as though I'm being forced out of town," she murmured as she turned away from her own face.

The ride across town was quick. Silke drove expertly, smoothly. Everything she did, she tried to do well. The club was a blaze of lights, laughter, and movement. Closing night was about to begin. Her mask in place, Silke guided the Jag up to the main portico. The valet rushed to the car, opening the door and smiling appreciatively as her bare legs slipped out. His hand was there in a gesture he rarely offered other women, young or old. Silke smiled at him as she rose gracefully from the low-slung car.

"Thank you, Mike," she murmured huskily.

"Any time, Silke," he replied before taking her place in the Jag. He might treat other cars with a young man's curiosity and need to speed, but not Silke's Jag. That he treated with respect and care because, in spite of what everyone said about her, he liked her. She didn't treat him like a thing, a piece of furniture. She looked at him when she spoke to him. She had noticed the cold he had had last year. And she even dropped a little extra in his hand every Christmas.

Unaware of Mike's appreciation, Silke entered the foyer of the club. Heads turned. Her name came from three different directions and all the hails were male. Her smile flashed, her lashes dropped, and she went into her act for the last time.

"What took you so long?" Drew demanded, reaching her first, his date trailing behind.

"I had to make myself beautiful," Silke purred.

Ricky joined them and wrapped an arm around Silke's waist, nudging her hip with his. The signal was so natural only he and Silke knew what it meant. "Sorry, old man, this night is mine."

Drew glared at his rival.

Ricky nodded toward the woman behind him. "Besides, you have your own lady."

Silke cast a swift, discreet look over the other woman before leaning into Ricky's side. "You should have picked me up at home," she murmured, ignoring the other couple.

He looked into her eyes, playing the game. "I couldn't get away. Besides, I'll make it up to you tonight."

She pouted at him, urging him away from the crowd that was gathering to go into the main room where dinner would be served. "I'd rather you made it up to me now."

Ricky lowered his head just enough to hiss, "Will you turn down the voltage, Silke?" He guided them to a secluded alcove, making sure her back was to the open area so that he could watch for anyone taking undue interest in their activities.

Her smile was dangerous, to match the mood she was in. She hated decisions being made for her, even when they were the right ones. "I'm just doing my job."

"You're just getting even," he replied with a sigh. "Will it make you feel any better to know that Hollander really is going to miss your help? We all are."

She searched his eyes, even as she molded her body to his. He could have been made of plaster for all the interest she had in the position and the man. "Do you mean that?"

"Every one of us means it. Until you gave us a way in, we hadn't been able to get near this group and they're some of the biggest single users in the city. They're also so certain that they have a handle on their supplier that they talk when they should be afraid to open their mouths." He bent his head to nuzzle her neck. "You opened the door, Silke. And if everything goes the way we expect, we'll have the head man in a week, if not sooner. We're setting up the sting now."

Triumph and satisfaction were better than meat and drink. Silke fed on them, for one moment the darkness of her past just a little lighter. "Just make sure you get them all." She lifted her lips for his kiss, which came and went with all the excitement of kissing her own hand.

Ricky lifted his head, smiling at her, genuine liking in his eyes for an instant. "Hollander thinks we should have a very public fight tonight. Something along the lines of my demanding that you stay here and you hating having me hanging on to your neck like a wet rag."

She grimaced delicately even as she considered the plan and found it workable. "Hollander's use of the king's English isn't mine. But I get the idea." She slipped her fingers through his hair. "How soon?"

"You decide. We want to make it so you won't be fending off some fool trying to take my place in your bed tonight. And heavy enough so that when I start bringing your replacement in, one of our regulars, no one will think it odd."

"All right. Give me about two hours. In that time, I ought to be able to stir up enough action in the male quarter to make it look good." She sighed deeply, even as she mentally reviewed the list of people who would be in the main room. No matter how many games she played, if anyone knew what to look for, they would realize she chose her players with skill. No one who was paired with one who mattered to him, no one who saw her as more than a body to be scored on an invisible tally sheet was ever selected for participation. Out of necessity to clean up her particular corner of the world, she used people, but only those tough enough to survive her influence or those who used others themselves.

The evening went exactly as she and Ricky planned. The fight was public enough to suit anyone's taste and was sure to figure in the gossip columns in the morning. Another mark against her with her family. Silke returned home, wrung out by the encounter. She turned on the stereo in the empty apartment, made herself a cup of tea, turned out the lights so that she could watch the stars and the moon from the open window in the living room. It was almost three. She ought to be in bed but she knew it would be a waste of time. Sleep was always elusive at this hour. Below her, the city stretched, murmured with the voices of those who inhabited the night. Danger lurked beneath the benevolence of the silver light of the moon. But not here, in this candy floss world of satin sheets, designer gowns, and rare scents. Tomorrow she would start a new life. But what did she want of it, of herself? Her crusade, the driving force of her adult life, was almost over, would be won by others than herself. She felt empty, lonely. Not new feelings, only stronger aches.

And what of her family? What had she done to them with her choices? What had they suffered? Until this moment, she hadn't allowed herself to think of that, because to acknowledge the cost they paid would have meant she would never have embarked on her course. Another debt to be settled. But how? She frowned in the darkness, for a moment remembering the winter lake eyes of the stranger, eyes burning with a contempt almost as strong as the desire in them. Strange how well she could remember him when she had barely allowed herself to notice him at the time. She shifted in her chair, her skin flushing with the memory of how he had seen her act. She knew all the tricks, to attract, to seduce. Being taught something almost from the cradle made impressions that would always remain.

"What good will a new life do me, if I take the old me along?" she asked the silence. "Will other men look at me and see what the stranger saw, judge as he judged, condemn without hearing the truth?" She shivered, realizing just what the next year might bring. She knew her position as one of the heirs to the St. James fortune had given her more than a measure of insulation from the slings and arrows of those who would have denounced her.

Lorraine had offered her a challenge. Could she accept in the fullness of the word? Could she truly make a clean break, leave the old Silke behind? She finished the last of her tea and set the cup aside. There was no other choice. The debt to the past was close to being paid. That had a high price tag. But tomorrow, she was going to pay an even higher one. She would tell her parents enough of the truth of the last few years. They deserved her honesty. The risk she was taking was great, but she accepted that as she had accepted the other chances she had taken. She had lived on the edge all of her life, stayed true to herself when to betray her own honor would have been easier and safer. She could do no less now.

"Yes, what is it, Grimes?" Lorraine asked, looking up from her perusal of the morning news and the latest of Silke's escapades.

"Miss Silke is here, Madam."

Lorraine's brows rose at the information. She glanced at Geoffrey, then at the tidbit they had both already read that had outlined in detail Silke's behavior at the club last night. "Ask her to come up, Grimes," she murmured.

Silke entered the sitting room that her mother and father had shared for breakfast each morning for as long as Silke had lived in this house. It was her parents' private time in a life filled to the brim with social, professional, and personal engagements. Only on rare occasions was anyone allowed to disturb them here. She stepped just inside as Grimes closed the door behind her. The newspaper lying open on the table beside them told her she was too late. Sighing, she moved toward the table. The disappointment in Lorraine's and Geoffrey's faces was there, partially masked but visible.

"I had hoped to get to you before you saw that," she said quietly, taking a seat across from them.

"Was it reported in error?" Lorraine asked, one brow arched in elegant curiosity.

Silke shook her head. "No. It's accurate, if slightly colored with drama." She searched their faces, seeing sadness rather than the condemnation that others would have given if confronted with the same situation. "I came to explain if you'll let me."

"Explain?" Lorraine glanced at Geoffrey to find him looking as surprised as she felt at the unexpected development.

Silke grimaced. "I know it's a shock. After we reached our majority, you've never demanded that any of us explain away our behavior."

"Daughter, I don't know what to say," Geoffrey said when Lorraine made no move to interrupt.

Silke waved the comment away. "Just listen, please." She

touched her mother's hand while she looked at her father. "Like you've always done. I can't tell you everything. In fact, I shouldn't be telling you anything at all, and if anything I do say leaves this room, people, myself included, will be in grave danger."

Geoffrey straightened in his chair, an aging eagle with enough power still to face a threat uncowed. "What are you into, child? Do we need Simpson in on this?" he asked bluntly, naming the family lawyer.

Lorraine edged forward in her seat, disturbed by the deadly seriousness of Silke's voice. It was a tone neither had ever heard.

"No." Silke paused, then said, "No matter how it has looked over these last four years, I haven't done anything illegal. In fact, just the opposite. I've been helping the drug enforcement people collect information on one of the biggest dealers in the state."

"Silke!" Lorraine breathed in horror, hardly noticing that Geoffrey had taken her other hand and was holding it tightly.

"Don't look like that, Mother. Other than the damage done to my reputation, I've been safe. After all, who would expect a woman with a reputation for crawling into half the male beds in the city, a lush besides, to have any thoughts in her head besides sex and where her next drink was coming from?" Anger and bitterness shaded the silence that followed.

"It isn't true? Your reputation, I mean?" Lorraine whispered, shocked, praying Silke was telling her the truth, horrified at the reality and the risks she had run.

"No, it isn't true," Silke replied gently, squeezing her mother's hand. She looked into Lorraine's eyes, finding the love she didn't deserve, the acceptance. "I can't tell you why I did it. But I can tell you that it mattered more to me to do this than anyone or anything. A few years ago, I stumbled into the situation, discovered things I shouldn't have, and started digging. Then I made some anonymous calls and that started the ball rolling. For a while, that's all I did. Then one day, a man approached me to make a drug buy. Everyone in my crowd knew I supposedly preferred the bottle to the powder, so I was suspicious. I won't tell you how, but I managed to find out who he was and who he worked for. In the end I worked for the same man and we all had one goal. Bring down the head man and destroy the network in this area. Now, they want me out of here. The goal we've all worked to achieve is in sight and my boss wants to tie up all the loose ends. Your idea is giving me a way out of here. That," she nodded toward the paper, "was the way we chose to cut the contact between me and my current partner."

"Current partner?" Geoffrey watched Silke's face as he asked the question.

"Three of my six engagements were partners as well. The other three were camouflage."

Lorraine stared, hardly able to take in the scope of all that Silke had been doing.

"You couldn't tell us?" Geoffrey asked finally.

Silke felt his hurt, absorbed it without trying to deny it. "For myself I would have. But I couldn't risk the rest of the team."

"Why now?"

"You've offered me a new life. And I have done what I must here with this one. I've hurt you and Mother when all you have ever done was love me. I don't have the right to ask you to forgive me, and I'm not. But I can give you the truth and I can tell you that I am going to take this new chance you're offering me and be someone you can be proud of. I won't take what I am here to Atlanta, not that it will mean the mud won't stick anyway. But I can guarantee you that I won't be bringing any more dirt to the family name. It won't make up for the disgrace I have brought to your name, but you have my word there will be no more from me."

Geoffrey shook his head, feeling his years as never before. "I don't know what to say, my dear. I can't deny that I have been hurt, as your mother has. I can't deny that the rumors, the gossip, and your name in the papers in the worst possible way most of the time have been very unpleasant. But knowing you were, probably still are, in danger isn't much better."

"You took such risks, Silke. Why?" Lorraine asked urgently.

"That I can't give you, Mother. Ask anything else of me but that." She met Lorraine's eyes, silently begging for her understanding. "It's over. I did what I had to do and it's over."

Lorraine searched Silke's face, seeing strength she had somehow missed in this daughter of her heart. She had thought C. R. the strongest of the four, but she now knew her error. Whatever lay in Silke's continued silence about her past, she suddenly knew must stay buried. Tears welled in her eyes. Although she had never lived the dark side of life, her years with the facility had opened her mind to what atrocities could be perpetrated on the weak, the vulnerable.

Silke's face changed when she saw the moisture. Pain such as she rarely felt threatened her composure. No one had ever cried over her. "Don't do that, Mother," she pleaded huskily.

Lorraine rose and held out her arms. Silke got up without even being aware that she moved, and walked into her embrace. The old and the young. The privileged and the deprived. For this moment in time, the differences were washed away in tears of love, and the past, present, and future shone for a brief illusionary instant, intact and unblemished.

"We can't do this," Lorraine objected. "You heard Silke. She says the danger leaves when she leaves town. You can't betray her confidence by telling Killian."

Geoffrey faced his wife, his mind made up. "Maybe, but I won't send our daughter to a strange city, away from whatever protection we can provide, without doing something to help. I'm not going to tell Killian the truth. We'll make use of Silke's reputation and endow her with an obsessive boyfriend or something like that."

Lorraine frowned worriedly. "But she wants to start a new life. A clean life."

"Killian knows all about her. We can't change that. But we can make sure Killian knows she's in danger. To hell with her reputation. Now, we both know it's a lie. This family can take the heat. We've certainly had our share or two of black sheep."

"You're beginning to sound like Silke. You make it sound so simple and we both know it isn't. What if these people try to hurt her? I saw Killian's face. I know he took Silke from someone else so that he could handle her case himself. He doesn't respect her, doesn't like her either." Lorraine massaged her temples. "Maybe we should call the whole thing off."

Geoffrey sat down on the couch and took Lorraine's hands in his. "We can't do that. Think of the questions it would bring up, my dear. Silke needs a legitimate way out of town and we can give her that. And no matter what Killian does or doesn't think, he will do his job. We can trust him."

"We are trusting him. With our daughter's life."

Killian watched Silke take leave of her parents from his position behind the column far away to their right. Ostensibly, he was reading the newspaper he held, but in reality he was watching the obvious love that flowed between the trio. The other three daughters had already departed on their respective planes. Silke was the last, probably given the latest flight because of her sleeping habits, he thought cynically.

Killian shifted restlessly, his gaze focused on a Silke he had yet to see. This one was softer, younger somehow than the others. She was dressed for comfort rather than attraction, and yet even the man's tailored shirt and safari tan slacks she wore didn't disguise the woman beneath the ordinary fabrics. Her skin glowed and this time he couldn't see any evidence of the cosmetic allure she had displayed at the party that night. Her hair was still imprisoned, fire tamed by her hand, drawing the eye and enticing the senses. He sighed deeply as he felt his body sing with enjoyment of the picture she presented, the obvious love she showed the pair who had lifted her out of the darkness of her past. How could two so divergent pictures reflect the same woman? Confusion was as new to him as the other emotions this woman seemed to invoke just by breathing in his presence. He didn't like unanswered questions, and he definitely didn't like items that didn't add up correctly. Silke should have fit into her slot. Instead she was rearranging his thinking, making him doubt his own judgments and perceptions. It was not a comfortable sensation, nor one he had ever experienced to this degree. Added to that, she didn't have the least idea of the glitch she had thrown his way. Of all of the above, the last was the most irritating, Killian acknowledged silently as he watched Silke start down the boarding tunnel.

Tucking his paper under his arm, he entered the corridor behind Silke, making certain that he appeared so engrossed in his thoughts that he didn't notice his friends, the St. Jameses. If there was an onlooker, specifically Silke's stalker, he wanted as few connections as possible between him and Silke at this point.

Besides, he really did have a lot to think about. With Geoffrey's announcement this morning, most of his game plan had been thrown out the window. The chances of his being able to watch Silke from a reasonable distance were being reduced by the moment with the danger that might just be following her to Atlanta. The fact that she had seen him at that party was an added complication. And the three thousand dollars which would only allow for the most basic accommodations if Silke even knew how to find such a thing. He settled into his seat, silently cursing this assignment for the mare's nest it was turning out to be.

Silke looked up from the fashion magazine she was trying to read as the plane dropped into another air pocket. So far the ride had been far from pleasant. First, her seat mate had tried to strike up a conversation, then the weather had turned nasty, bouncing the plane around more than most of the other passengers liked. Everyone was belted up for safety and today's flight seemed to be crowded to overflowing with children, all in various forms of temper. The three in front of her were causing the least trouble, although for the last few minutes the youngest had been crying noisily and continuously.

"Shut up, kid," the man beside Silke muttered irritably, casting the baby a nasty look.

Silke tucked the magazine in the pocket in front of her and leaned forward. "May I help?" she asked quietly, pitching her voice to a soft croon. The squalling baby on the harassed mother's shoulder was staring at her, its mouth agape for another yell.

Silke stroked the damp cheek, smiling at the cross face. "Hi, little man. Want to come play with me?"

The baby sucked in air. The passenger next to Silke grimaced. The mother glanced over her shoulder, her pretty face a picture of surprise. "I really couldn't let you. Besides, Danny hates strangers."

"But I'm not a stranger, am I, honey?" Silke held out her hands to the toddler.

Danny, for reasons best known to himself, gave her a toothless grin and lifted his arms.

"I really don't mind and you have more than enough to do with the other two."

The woman frowned doubtfully. "You're sure?"

Silke's seat mate scowled irritably. "Lady, give her the kid. I don't know about the rest of the plane, but this damn ride is bad enough without those kids screaming. I've got to work when we finally land. Have a heart."

Silke could cheerfully have kicked the man, but that was scarcely behavior guaranteed to endear her to a nervous mother.

Danny settled the question for everyone concerned. He had the pretty lady's attention and he was keeping it. Squirming, he grabbed for the slender hands held out to him, holding on with all his sticky-fingered strength. Then he pulled, yanking himself up and over the back of the seat before anyone could stop him. Silke had no choice. She caught him as he launched himself arrow-straight at her chest.

Danny tipped back his head, giving Silke a triumphant grin, instantly making baby conversation.

"I guess you know what you want," Silke murmured to the child just as the plane dropped without warning again. Danny clutched at her, his smile dying. She cradled him close, whispering nonsense.

Sitting two rows back, on an aisle seat as Silke was, Killian stared at Silke, stunned both at her offer and at the way she was holding the child. He would have bet his last dime that she not only didn't know anything about children but had even less interest in them. It didn't seem to be bothering her a bit that the baby was drooling all over her shoulder and yanking on her hair. She was smiling, smiling as he had never seen her. Softly, gently, her eyes glowing with tenderness. Where was the temptress? he wondered. The woman who could seduce a man in his dreams? He hardly noticed the bumpy flight, the escalating complaints of the passengers, the few who got sick as he watched Silke amuse the child, ignore the disgruntled man beside her and the jarring ride. But when his acute hearing picked up the sound of her humming softly, he was past surprise. Her voice wasn't strong but somehow it was soothing, not only to the baby perched on her shoulder but to those around her. Mr. Uncongeniality settled down with a sigh, managing to look peacefully inclined. The mother and two children in the seats in front of Silke stopped shifting around, and Danny poked his thumb in his mouth and went to sleep. Everyone seemed to breathe a sigh of relief with the quiet, and when the seat belt sign finally went off, normality was restored.

"May I get you something to drink?" the flight attendant asked, stopping beside him.

Killian gave his order without taking his eyes from Silke and the child.

"She's marvelous with him, isn't she?" the woman murmured, glancing briefly over her shoulder. "I didn't think he'd ever settle."

Killian inclined his head without giving a direct answer. He was still adding up the sum of one Silke Brown-St. James. The total was neither expected nor the same any two times running. And that bothered him. His experiences had taught too many lessons. Every human being had certain characteristics, traits that followed them through time, whether they were murderer or hero. Silke wasn't staying true to her traits. Party girls did not care that a child needed soothing. Of course, one could argue that even the worst of humanity often had a saving grace or two. Perhaps that was it.

Four

Silke glanced past her seat mate to the window, murmuring to Danny as the plane made its touchdown. The toddler dug his hands in her hair, a favorite game he had been playing for the last ten minutes. She smiled at him as the aircraft began taxiing toward the terminal. Leaning back in her seat, she held him close for the final few minutes, liking the feel of his sturdy little body, even the drooling smile and hot-fingered clutches he continued to bestow on her.

"I don't know what I would have done without you," Danny's

mother murmured ruefully, turning slightly in her seat so that she could look at Silke.

"Are you being met?" Silke asked, interrupting what sounded like an elongated thanks.

"Oh, yes. My husband has been transferred here. He'll be waiting for us." She unfastened her seat belt and started to get up, holding out her arms for her child.

"I don't mind carrying him for you." She nodded toward the other two small children and the crowd of passengers filling the aisle.

"I couldn't let you."

Silke grinned, not the seductive smile that usually gained her ends, but rather an uncomplicated woman-to-woman exchange. "How about if I take the choice out of your hands and just keep him until your husband can take over?" she suggested.

The other woman laughed. "All right." She tucked one hand of each of her other children into hers. "But don't you think we should at least exchange names?"

"I'm Silke."

"What a lovely name. It suits you, too. Mine's Maggie."

They were standing now, waiting for the way to clear enough for them to exit. Killian listened and watched the two, using the pretense of getting his briefcase and papers together. They were an unlikely pair, Maggie the mother and Silke the seductress.

"Do you live in Atlanta?" Maggie asked.

"No, just moving here."

"A job?"

Silke shook her head, surprised how little she minded Maggie's questions. She had spent a lifetime keeping her own counsel. Perhaps it was because she wouldn't be seeing Maggie again that she could let down her guard.

"Friends?"

"No." Silke grinned at the ready sympathy in Maggie's eyes. "Don't look so worried. I make friends easily."

Maggie grinned back, her eyes twinkling. "I can imagine you would, especially male friends." Seeing the aisle relatively clear, she edged into the corridor.

Silke joined her.

"You must meet my husband. His company is expanding here

and he's the personnel officer. I know they're hiring but I don't know what kind of jobs. It might not be something you're interested in but . . ." Maggie's words trailed off, a faint hint of pink running under her clear skin. "Or maybe you already have other arrangements."

"Actually I don't," Silke admitted, thinking quickly. She was too intent on the unexpected bonus Maggie had just offered and the baby she held to notice the man who turned his back to them as they moved down the aisle to the exit. "And I would appreciate talking to your husband. But I warn you, about the only thing I'm good for is answering a phone and planning parties." As they talked, they entered the tunnel leading to the waiting area.

Maggie frowned. "But surely you've had jobs?"

Silke shook her head. "I've spent most of my time doing volunteer work and going to school and, before you ask, getting a degree that probably has little or no application in the job market."

"I'm being pushy again," Maggie muttered, embarrassed. "Mickey says my mouth runs on wheels. I'm sorry."

Silke laughed, a husky flow of sound that turned heads. Danny gurgled, tapping her cheek with one pudgy hand. At that moment, a masculine voice hailed them.

Maggie's face lit up as did her children's. Silke followed the other woman more slowly, allowing the reunion to happen without her. When Maggie emerged from her husband's arms, she was laughing, talking too fast, words tumbling over each other.

"I don't think she ever shuts up," Mickey said fondly, extending his hand to Silke, introducing himself a second later.

Danny lunged at his father, babbling baby nonsense. Everyone dived for him but Mickey ended up with the prize.

"I thought I had dropped him," Silke said, shaking her head. "He's fast."

Killian stood off to the right, half hidden by the people milling between him and Silke. So far he had managed to stay out of her range of sight. But now came the tricky part. Like her, he had a car waiting in the parking lot, but after that there were no more easy connections between them. He could easily follow her to wherever she chose for an apartment, since he had a homing device attached to each of the four cars allotted to the daughters. But even with the electronic tracker, Silke still had a whole city in which to find a job, get an apartment, and make friends. If he intended to be her guard, he had to get close in all three. Thinking hard, he studied the couple who apparently were prepared to befriend her. His eyes narrowed as he focused on the man, who, until now, had been nothing more than a figure. There was something familiar about his face. A second later he remembered. Unless he was very much mistaken, that was Mickey Douglas, younger brother to one of his best friends. He hadn't seen Mickey in ten years, at least, but he had kept in touch with his older brother, the owner of the company for which Mickey worked. Spike could be trusted with enough of his reasons for being in town to get him at least one of the connections he needed, maybe even two. But that still left the living arrangements to worry about. With the threat of a stalker hanging over Silke's head, he wanted a place as close to her apartment as he could get, preferably in the same building or on the same floor.

Silke studied the directions that Mickey had written down for her, frowning at the unfamiliar names. This new life business was already showing some gaps in her knowledge. For one thing she seemed to have a rotten sense of east and west. She knew she was practically on top of the apartment complex that Mickey and Maggie had recommended. But so far all she had done was turn down the wrong streets, pass the same buildings, and in general waste gas and time. The latter she could afford, but the former was making a hole in her budget. Three thousand dollars wasn't all that much to get set up with when one had only the clothes on one's back and not a thing with which to keep house—or even a house to keep.

"Oh well," she muttered. "I've done crazier things. Nobody said this would be easy." She eased back into traffic and decided she'd make one more attempt before she stopped for a hamburger. "If only my 'friends' could see me now." Grinning, she turned up the radio and rolled down the window. The wind whipped through her hair. Suddenly she felt free. The feeling wouldn't last, but she intended to enjoy it while it did. Tomorrow and all its problems would arrive soon enough.

* * *

"Where is that nutty woman going now?" Killian said under his breath, handling his car with a lot more respect for the traffic than Silke had so far shown. Evening was waltzing slowly around the city, lighting streetlights, blurring the glare of the sun, tinting pink the gray haze that seemed to be Atlanta's habitual shroud. "I heard those directions, you crazy woman. There is no way you can keep missing the turn." He glared at Silke's car. He was hungry. If he intended to have a bed sometime tonight, he'd better do something. Accelerating, he shot around Silke's car, leaving enough room for safety but not enough so that she wouldn't have to slow down. The turn that she wanted, marked by a sign half obscured by a tree, was just ahead. He slammed on his brakes as though he just noticed it, watched her do the same and suddenly see the sign. He released his breath in a gust of air and headed for the first groups of slots in front of the manager's office. Silke pulled in right beside him.

He got out without appearing to notice her. He knew the moment she recognized him but he kept on walking.

Silke stared at the lean man with the lazy stride that seemed to eat up the distance between the cars and the apartment complex office. It wasn't possible. The stranger who had stared at her so intently that night was in Atlanta. "What is he doing here?" she muttered to herself, following him to the office door. She stopped abruptly as he opened the door for her to precede him. His blue eyes were no less intense than they had been the night of the party. Nor were they any less searching, seeming to catalogue her features and figure with one look. Irritated, off balance in a way she never was, Silke stared back at him for a moment, paused half in and half out of the entrance.

"You're blocking the way," Killian murmured softly. His fantasies hadn't lied. This woman was lethal. Up close, her sensuality was even more potent. Her scent, that tormentor of his recent dreams, once again demanded attention, wrapping around him with invisible fingers, stroking his desire, lighting fires that he had no intention of allowing to blaze.

"I know you," Silke returned just as softly.

He smiled faintly, then laughed, the effort surprisingly costly. "Do you get many men with that line?"

Silke wasn't thrown by that smile, as charming and sexy as it

was. Men lied with their expressions; most of them were even
better at it than women. But eyes held truth. And this man's eyes
held no amusement, only a searching quality that stripped her of
pretense, of masks, of games. He was dissecting her. And although
he didn't admit he remembered her, she knew that he did. This
was not a man who would forget anything or anyone unless it
suited him to do so.

He was tall, six one or two. She had been right about his eyes.
They were the color of a mountain lake in winter, deep blue, icy
calm. His hair was ebony, a raven wing shade that was rich enough
to invite a woman's fingers to play in the strands. Without realizing it, she leaned toward him slightly, delicately testing his scent,
not the expensive cologne he wore, but rather the basic male fragrance that commanded her senses to inhale, absorb, taste, and
savor. She approved. For the first time in her life, she felt desire
for someone. Deep, sharp, and compelling. Her brows rose, her
need tearing at the control that had always been hers. She held
his eyes, looking beyond the calm surface to the seething caldron
below. Anger, bone deep and soul wide. Shocking. Cruel. Contempt unmasked. Determination. Denial. She blinked, drawing
back, caught off guard by what she found, felt. A new life, she
reminded herself, shutting down her responses, damming her need,
cooling her thinking.

"Do you fool many women with that smile?" she retaliated
slowly, her gaze as analytical as his own.

Killian stared at her. For long moments, she had delved into
his soul, known his secret need for her, read what he would have
sworn was known to him alone. No woman, no man had ever had
that power. Anger came, cleansing, hungry. He had always been
a watcher of humanity, not a participant. He liked his choices,
his way of life. With one look, this lightweight piece of fluff had
cut through to his core, making a lie of his judgment of her and
a lie of his assessment of himself.

"A few," he admitted, giving her honesty he wouldn't have
offered the day before. "There are always people around who
accept the face without worrying or caring about what goes on
behind it." He shifted his stance, openly challenging her now.

Silke was a student of body language. Her survival had depended on her skill too often in the past for her ever to forget its

lessons. Yesterday, she would have taken him on, for the danger of the game, the high of the chase, the fire of the need. Today, she faced the challenge and did a mental retreat. She lifted one slim shoulder, the gesture having any meaning he cared to place on it. Then she turned her head, knowing he still watched her as she walked ahead of him into the room. She half expected him to speak but he didn't. He simply followed her, standing beside her as the formalities for rental were handled with a word to the manager because of the call that Mickey had placed on her behalf. She finished her paperwork before he did and turned to watch him, trying to figure out what he was doing here. She just didn't believe in this kind of coincidence.

"You're staring," Killian murmured, when the manager left them to get their keys.

Her eyes narrowed to tawny slits. "What are you doing in Atlanta?" Thanks to the manager's friendly comments to the man at her side, she had a name to attach to this male who watched her so carefully.

Killian leaned against the desk, letting male interest show. "Following you. Silke Brown-St. James." He put just enough glibness into the truth to make it unbelievable.

Her brows arched skeptically. "A stranger? For what reason?" He played a strange game with unusual answers but this was a new life, a different set of rules. His maleness seemed to flow out of his pores to touch her, to enfold her in need and seductive, beguiling warmth. Men had been figures in her life since she turned from child to woman. But not one had really reached her on the primitive level that commanded her own need. She had been wanted but never had she wanted, not like this, not a stranger, not a man who spoke one answer with his lips and another truth with his eyes. Danger. The word was more than jeopardy. It was a promise, present and future, that she couldn't afford. Not the man, the challenge, or the high of danger dared. Her life was made up of hard choices, impossible choices. Killian Carpenter had just become another of those choices, a sacrifice to her own peace, a peace she intended to have at last, now that her debts were paid. So she looked at him, felt the sword of desire slide through her, wounding, taking without giving back. Then she pulled out the blade, not easily, not even willingly but definitely.

She had come to start fresh. She would succeed with that if with nothing else.

"Obvious ones, I would have thought."

Killian saw that awareness of him as a man one more time in her eyes. He waited, expecting anything and nothing. Silke was already teaching him that rules had little meaning to her. His body liked her look, too much. It preened, blood rushing to the parts of him that wished a more intimate acquaintance. Time seemed to cease, his breathing was matched with the rise and fall of her breasts beneath the thin man's shirt she wore as though it were a designer gown. Then, as swiftly as the awareness came, Silke turned from it and him, her slender body showing no signs of the arousal that was even now an insistent pain. She had seen. She had conquered, and she had walked away. Killian thrust his hands in his pockets and cursed silently, cursed himself for goading her, cursed her for retaliating, and cursed his own ego that felt the slap of Silke's silent rejection.

"Here you are," the manager said as he returned to hand each a key.

Silke took her key without looking at Killian, thanked the man, and headed for the door. She still had a lot to do—too much perhaps—but it would keep her mind occupied. She didn't hear Killian follow her. Only when he covered her hand with his when she reached to open her car door did she realize he was there. Startled, she yanked her fingers back, turning to face him at the same time.

"What do you want?"

"Company for dinner. I don't know anyone here. Do you?"

"Maybe."

"Do you have plans?" He tucked his hands in his pockets, watching her closely. This wasn't how he had envisioned this assignment, but he had to play the cards he had been dealt.

"Not the kind you mean. I intend to have an early night."

"On what?"

She frowned at him. "What do you mean, on what? A bed of course."

"You have a hotel room?"

She thought fleetingly of her meager cash, more than half of which she had just given to the apartment manager. "I just rented an apartment."

"An unfurnished apartment."

"So?"

"No bed."

"Now that depends on your definition of a bed, doesn't it?" she murmured, copying Noelle's best vague tone.

Killian's eyes narrowed in assessment. "Meaning?" His tone was rougher than he wanted, more telling. The game was suddenly real.

Silke met his look, her own no less straight. "My business."

"Woman, did anyone ever tell you that cryptic answers tend to irritate?"

"Do I look as if I care whether you're ready to chew nails or not?" She opened her car door, standing inside it as she turned to him again. "I don't know what you want of me. It isn't because you're interested in me in the normal man-woman way. And even if you were, I don't want you."

"So you lie?" Black brows peaked over eyes that dared her to deny that twice she had found him attractive, that she had wanted him.

Silke didn't like corners, especially when she was in one. "All right, I don't want to want you and I won't."

"That could be a challenge." He shook his head when she opened her mouth to respond. "I asked you to share a meal with me. That's all."

"Nothing is ever that simple, even with a simple man, which you are far from being."

"You can tell that from just a few minutes of conversation?"

"I read people well."

He took a step closer, caging her with his body in the open car door. "Then read this. Whether I like you or not, I want to see you again and, with us living on the same floor, apartment mates if you need a label, I will see you, talk to you, think about you." If Killian had been thinking about his job, he would have shut up long before he reached this stage of his usually controlled temper. But Silke had caught him unaware of his own need.

Silke searched his hard face, the shadowed angles and planes that spoke silently of experiences learned in a hard school and memories that carried enough pain to score the cup of his emotions. He wasn't a gentle man and, so far, certainly not an honest one with her. But right this instant, he was telling the truth. He wanted her. Sex was driving him, and he wanted a chance to see if it would drive her, too.

"No, Killian."

Simple denial without emotion to cloud it. Killian had thought he could goad her into lowering her guard. If she had been who he had believed her to be, the tactic should have succeeded. Because it did not, he frowned, rearranging his thinking yet again.

"If I promise, only a meal?" Aggression hadn't hooked her. Finesse might.

She smiled faintly. "No, Killian. No meal. No me. No you. No us. Simple. I'm here to learn to be good. You were at the party. You think I'm that woman."

"Show me you're not then." He curved his hands about her shoulders, surprised at how delicate her bones felt in his grasp.

"A devil's lure. It won't work. The only one I have to show is myself and maybe those who love me. And you fit neither of those categories." She raised her hands and circled his wrists, lifting up. Heat burned where his fingers had touched her. She ignored the sensation as she was determined to ignore the man. "Now go away. You won't push me into accepting what I don't want. You won't trick me into it either. Only honesty works."

"Do you give honesty to others?"

The question hit hard, but Silke didn't dodge the strike. "To those who matter to me, yes."

Silke sat down on the seat, swung her legs beneath the steering wheel, and shut the door. She didn't look at Killian as she started the car, reversed, and drove slowly out of the small lot to find her apartment at the rear of the complex. She knew Killian would follow. He had no choice, for as he said, he was sharing the second floor of the two-story quads that dotted the area with its man-made lakes, carefully tended landscape, and community pool and tennis court. The amenities lifted it above the average but not so far that Silke couldn't afford the rest with her limited budget.

But even as she appreciated the setting, she didn't forget the man who embodied all that she had left behind. She had put her foot on the path of her new life. She hadn't counted on having part of the old follow her steps.

"He won't win," she muttered as she parked her car and got out without looking around. "He won't win."

Five

Killian glared at the empty apartment even as he kept his ear, figuratively, glued to the door. He had to know the moment Silke left her place. Whether she wanted him or not, he couldn't let her wander around on her own. He frowned as he considered the moments he had spent with her. She was definitely nothing like her dossier proclaimed her to be or the way that he had seen her act. For one thing, there was a mind in that exquisite body. There was also depth and perception. All three surprised him. But what surprised him more was that she would turn away from the desire they had both felt. If it had been one half as strong for her as for him, she shouldn't have wanted to do that, probably wouldn't even have been able to . . . if, that is, she was the woman she was supposed to be.

Puzzles. Of all the human equation, those intrigued him the most. And this woman shouldn't be a puzzle. She should have been as easy to read as her blatant attempts that night at the party to attract the male.

"Damn her," he muttered, using up yet another of his curses. "Which one is the real Silke and which the lie? Both can't exist in the same female."

The sound of a door closing pushed him into action. Killian left his apartment, moving swiftly enough to catch Silke at the stairs.

Silke glanced over her shoulder and sighed. "I knew it was too good to be true."

"We both have to eat. I hate doing it alone." He shrugged, matching his pace to hers as they walked down. She was so close he could have touched her with very little effort. But he didn't make that effort, despite the fact that his body wanted that contact very much. Instead, he concentrated on her mind, the person, trying to find at least one answer in the sea of questions that surrounded her.

Silke considered the flat reply, hearing the purpose that lay just below the surface. She knew the value of patience, of seeming to bow to the inevitable when no other course was apparent. She also knew the value of timing. "So you're going to follow me to a restaurant or whatever?"

Killian met her eyes, noting but not reacting to the challenge in her stance and her demand. "Yes," he said neutrally.

Her brows arced, her lips twitching slightly at the corners. Honesty had always held its own kind of fascination, a silent allure that few men realized was seductive. "I didn't expect you to admit it," she said after a second.

"Whenever possible, I prefer truth to lies," he replied, stopping on the sidewalk.

Silke halted in front of him, measuring the man and his words. Perhaps he was different. Perhaps he would not continue to judge her because of their one meeting. Perhaps she could risk just one meal with him. "How long is this going to go on?"

One brow lifted. "What 'this' are we talking about?"

"Chasing me."

"I thought I was being friendly."

"Truth. Remember?"

He looked away for a second, considering his options. There weren't that many. "I want to get to know you," he answered finally, looking back at her in time to catch her skeptical look. "You don't believe me."

"No. I know dislike when I see it, and I certainly can understand contempt. I saw both that night at the party." She had to be sure there was at least a chance for her to live above the reputation she had left behind. She had made promises, to herself and her parents.

"Maybe it was for the man you were with."

She studied him, probing what little he was allowing her to see. The very fact that he was camouflaging his reactions told her a lot. Wary, uneasy suddenly when a moment before she had been curious, she asked, "Was it?"

Killian almost made the mistake of lying. At the last second he changed his mind. "No. You played that fool like a fish on a hook. He didn't have the least idea what you are."

Mentally she drew back, hearing the contempt she had seen so vividly that night. "And you do?" she responded, bitter without realizing that she had betrayed her reaction.

Killian didn't need to hear it to feel it. "No. I thought I did," he admitted, making no attempt to blunt his assessment. "Now, I'm not sure and I want to be." He lifted his hand to her but didn't touch her. The job he had come to do drowned in the need he suddenly knew to reach her, touch her mind as he couldn't allow himself to touch her body. "You intrigue me. Too much for such a short acquaintance."

Silke had asked for truth. Looking at him, seeing the clear light in his eyes, hearing the words that mirrored her own emotions, she found what she sought. He had judged her. He had disliked what he had believed her to be, and still he wanted a chance to get close to her. Perhaps it was better this way. If Killian hadn't known what she was, she would have had to face the prospect of explaining herself at some point in the future, if there was a future. This way, he knew the bad up front.

But more than that, she needed some answers herself. Her senses were demanding that she listen to their needs for the first time in her life. Even now, she was aware of him in ways she had never known. The night was gentle, whispers of tomorrows drifting with the light breeze that caressed her skin. She had come to build a new life. She had thought to have time to become accustomed to this unknown future. Maybe the fates had other treats in store. Maybe it was time once again for her to take courage in hand and reach out for a star she hadn't thought could be hers.

A risk. But her life had always been that and she had survived.

"Does it take you that long to decide?" Killian asked, stroking her cheek with gentle fingers.

Silke blinked, focusing on his face, the faint smile that invited her nearer. She leaned an inch closer, then caught herself. A chance was one thing. Sheer recklessness something else entirely. She drew back, away from the warmth of his touch, the tenderness of his voice in the darkness.

"All right." Silke started for her car.

Killian stared after her for a second, then moved quickly to catch up. For one instant there had been a softness about her, a vulnerability that again didn't match the woman he had thought her to be. "What do you mean 'all right'?"

Silke didn't look at him. "I mean you can eat with me if you like. But I warn you, my budget doesn't stretch to anything but the first fast-food hamburger place I can find."

He caught her arm, swinging her around so that he could see her eyes. "My treat."

She shook her head. "My way or no way."

He laughed, surprised enough at the singsong delivery to forget his misconceptions, his job, and her physical appeal. Real liking slipped through all the rest, the good and the bad.

Her grin was young, oddly innocent for a woman who could be anything but that.

"All right. You win. This time." He urged her toward his car. "But I'm driving. I saw what you're like in this traffic."

"You have ketchup on your chin," Killian murmured.

Silke chuckled as she cleaned off the minuscule spot. "That's only fair. You have mustard on yours." She stabbed three more French fries into a pool of red and waved them at him. "I don't think I have ever met anyone who put mustard on fries before."

"At least it makes me memorable," he drawled, finishing off his meal. He couldn't remember the last time he had eaten in one of these places. And he certainly couldn't remember ever having such a strange companion to share his meal with. Silke should have looked out of place, but somehow she didn't. She had ordered her meal as though she had always eaten cheap food and then dug into the paper-wrapped feast as though it were filet mignon.

"You're staring again," she said, shaking her head. "What image am I not fitting this time?"

Startled, Killian didn't answer immediately. "What makes you ask a question like that?"

She shrugged. "You aren't all that hard to read. Besides, I already told you I'm good at it."

Killian could have told her just how difficult he was to understand, how few people he knew well, how few he wanted to know well.

"And you won't get away with a question to answer a question. I also have a better than average memory."

There was no harm in telling her. "You act as though you have done this all of your life."

"My history isn't any secret. I was thirteen when Lorraine and Geoffrey St. James adopted me."

"That had to have been a difficult age for you," he murmured.

Silke looked beyond him to the past she had willingly left behind, to the darkness that had almost captured her in its death grip. Even now, she couldn't believe she had actually escaped physically unscathed.

Killian inhaled sharply at the sudden shadows of pain in her eyes. Sometimes he could see nothing but what she let him see. Only rarely did she drop her guard enough to let him in, as she was doing now. It hurt. Too damn much for a man who was supposed to stay detached, objective. Before he could stop himself, he reached across the table and took her hand, his thumb stroking lightly over the delicate bones.

"Whatever it is, bury it again, Silke. It's over."

The curiously rough, soft words penetrated the mental night, bringing light, warmth. Silke blinked, coming back to the present and the unmasked concern glowing in his eyes. "You are not a fool. No part of us, no memory, is ever really buried or over," she said, pulling her hand from his.

"If you let it, it can be."

"Cut out part of what made me as I am?" Her brows rose at the thought. "Destroy the lessons that I've learned, the mistakes and the triumphs?" She shook her head. "No. That isn't my way. It will never be my way."

"It hurts you. I can see that."

"Yes. But I survived it, learned from it, gave to it, lived it. A part of me. Dark perhaps. But without dark to define the light, no picture, no image, can be made." She pushed the food away, suddenly no longer amused, relaxed. "I'm tired."

Killian got to his feet, knowing that he had stumbled badly and knowing, too, there would be no immediate retrieval of his position. "I'll take you home."

Silke didn't answer as she walked with him to the car. Killian drove and she was silent. He watched her but he doubted that she even realized that. He didn't understand what part of her he had touched, had hurt. The need to hold her, to promise her that he would not hurt her like that again was strong, but he controlled it. He had seen wounded animals fold in on themselves when the pain was too great to be touched. Silke was doing that now, suffering in a way in which he wouldn't have thought her capable. Only when they got out of the car did he speak.

"Where will you sleep?"

Silke glanced at him, hardly hearing the question. "On the floor. I've slept on worse. At least it isn't cold."

"Will a sleeping bag help?"

Startled, Silke asked, "You have one?"

He nodded.

"Then what will you use?"

"Same thing. I brought two just in case the heat wasn't on, but it is." He didn't wait for her agreement. He walked around to the trunk and pulled out one of the down bags and a pillow and tucked it under his arm. "I'll come back for my stuff after we get yours upstairs."

"I can manage."

"But you don't have to." He looked at her, daring her to argue.

Her lips twitched, life flowing back into her limbs. The past slipped away. "I'll owe you one then."

Killian took her keys from her and opened her trunk. "Good. You can pay me off tomorrow. I need help picking out some furniture. Not much to start until I get a job. I figure you're in the same boat from what I heard in Philly. So take pity on me and we'll hit the stores together."

The idea held appeal. More than it should have. Telling herself she was happy to be alone in a strange city only stretched so far. "Can't. I have a job interview in the morning."

"Where?" Killian pulled her two cases out of the car, keeping the heavier for himself.

"Douglas Plastics."

He smiled faintly, dropping into the role he had assigned himself. "So you're going to the new branch they're setting up here."

"You know them?" Silke led the way up the stairs.

"I should. The owner is a friend of mine. He said he might have a job for me."

Silke unlocked her door and preceded him inside. "Doing what?"

"We haven't discussed it yet. I was going to talk to him the day after tomorrow, but if you're going that way, why don't I go at the same time and then we'll hit the stores."

Silke dropped her case on the floor in the larger bedroom. "I'm beginning to believe you really are following me," she murmured, turning to search his face.

Killian met her look, letting her make her own decision. "Well?" he asked when she didn't say anything.

"All right. We'll do it that way." It was almost too easy to agree. The meal they had shared had created a comfortable ease she wanted to enjoy. With the exception of that brief stab of memory that hadn't really been Killian's fault, he had been kind, humorous, and easy to talk to. Besides, she wasn't all that calm about her first job application. Having company was definitely preferable to going in alone.

He smiled and closed the distance between them.

Silke was fast enough on the uptake to catch the swift change in his expression. Suddenly, male interest was alive and breathing fire. And she wasn't ready to be singed. Before he could touch her, she held him off with a hand against his chest. "But as friends."

"Friends?" He tasted the word and found its flavor strange on his tongue. The dominant part of his nature raised its head, alert, strong, and ready to do battle. He studied her expression, looking for but not finding one chink in her feminine armor.

Silke felt the war going on within him. Her nerves tightened, ready for defense. If he rushed her now, she would not let him close again. She would know that he believed the lies rather than bothering to look for the truth despite what his eyes had told him she was. Even as she formed the thoughts, she knew the burden she was placing on him was unfairly weighted. But fate and her own choices had decreed this confrontation. "Friends. Or nothing."

He read her look, knowing he had pushed as far as he dared. He didn't think she could cage her desire one bit better than he could his own. But she was right whether he wanted to admit it or not. He had cautioned his men against getting involved, and he had broken his own rule. "All right. Friends it is." He stepped back, out of temptation's way. "I'll pick you up at nine."

She grimaced at the early hour, suddenly wondering how she was going to hold down a nine-to-five job when she couldn't sleep like normal people.

"What's the frown for?"

She shook her head. "Nothing."

Killian studied her face, seeing what he hadn't seen before. Evasion. Something was wrong. "If you really don't want to do it this way, just say so."

"It isn't that." She bent down to unlock her case.

Killian squatted beside her, stopping her with a hand on hers. "I thought you believed in honesty."

"I do." She glanced at him and read the determination to know what had caused her change of expression. Sighing, she sat back on her heels. "You are the most infuriating man. I don't know why I let you badger me."

He grinned slightly, knowing that, against her better judgment, she was going to tell him whatever it was. "Maybe it's my winning personality." He touched her cheek. "Stop putting it off, whatever it is. Just tell me and I'll leave."

For the first time in her life, Silke felt the fool. No one, and that included her family, knew of the extreme difficulty she had in sleeping at night. "I'm a nocturnal creature. I don't sleep at night, because I can't."

Any amusement in Killian's expression died as he searched her eyes and found the truth. The agony he had briefly glimpsed was there as well. "Why?" The word was gentle. The need to know was not. Even as he spoke, his fingers traced the smooth curve of her cheek, testing the silky texture of her skin, the intriguing warmth.

Silke's lashes flickered. "I just can't, that's all."

She was lying. Killian shifted restlessly, wanting to confront her and knowing he would not, at least not yet. Whatever she was hiding was not something she would share with a man she wasn't even certain she trusted.

"Are you tired?"

Silke's lashes lifted quickly at the soft question. "No."

"Neither am I. I'll make you a deal. I'll help you set up your place here and then we'll work on mine. And after that, we'll find ourselves a twenty-four-hour market and get some food."

Silke stared at him, unable to believe he was serious.

Killian grinned at her surprise as he tapped the end of her nose with a gentle finger. A kiss on those delicious lips would have been much better, but he was getting a measure of this siren called Silke. She couldn't be rushed or seduced, and she was too honest to deserve trickery. She had made the rules. He didn't know why, and, oddly enough, he didn't want to make any guesses that might be wrong. So he'd play it her way until he had the answers he needed.

"Come on, sexy lady, let's get moving. Those hamburgers aren't going to hold me all night." He rose and headed for the door. "I'll leave you to unpack your frillies while I bring the rest of my stuff up."

Silke listened to the door close, her eyes still on the emptiness he had left behind. Without her knowing it, her hand crept up to cover the place where his fingers had traced her cheek. No one, not man, not parents, not sisters, not friends, had ever touched her so simply and yet so deeply. She, who believed in few gentle emotions, suddenly discovered tenderness, in his smile, his voice, and the light stroke of his hand. She was warm when she hadn't realized she was cold. She was less alone when she allowed herself to feel the fullness of her isolation from life. All because of one man, a stranger and yet not a stranger. She didn't notice the moments she spent staring at the doorway. When she heard his soft whistling as he passed her door on the way to his apartment, she realized how long she had been motionless. Shaking her head, smiling faintly at her own inexplicable reactions, she turned to her case. Her smile became a laugh as she poked through the contents. Every piece of sexy lingerie she possessed was tumbled in a silk and satin collage over her more carefully folded blouses and slacks.

"No wonder he said 'frillies.' "

"I don't suppose when you said 'friends,' you meant the intimate kind, the kind who could talk you into giving me a private show?" Killian asked as he propped himself against her bedroom door, his arms folded over his chest.

At the first sound of his voice, Silke looked up, her hands full of panties and bras. The teasing tone didn't match the very real male need in his eyes. When she only shook her head without saying a word, he pushed away from the door and came to her, kneeling beside her. "You were supposed to be done with those before I got back."

Silke's thoughts were uncharacteristically scrambled, but she managed to pull one coherent idea out. "There wasn't any place to put them."

"So you decided to hold them?" Black brows rose as he glanced at the bounty in her hands. "How about if I do that little job for you?" He slipped his fingers into the delicate mound, the silk, satins, and laces caressing his palms. Every plan to be objective and just friendly fled. She would be like this to caress—soft, delicate, smooth, and warm. He tangled his fingers with hers as he looked into her eyes. "I like your taste. . . ." he murmured huskily, his gaze on her mouth. "In clothes."

Silke felt the heat of his voice wrap around her, drawing her closer. He was a sorcerer with words, with vocal tones and textures, making love to her without ever touching her intimately. Her lips parted, her tongue tracing their fullness as his kiss would have done.

Desire was Silke—hot, wary, and demanding. Killian knew he was breaking her rules and his own. He knew suddenly he would go on breaking them. "Come closer," he commanded softly. He would not take, but he definitely would give.

Silke leaned toward him, lost in the maze he had brought her to and trod with her. Lingerie dropped into his lap unheeded by either of them. He drew her nearer, still holding her hands rather than drawing her into his arms.

"One kiss."

Silke stared at his mouth, wanting it as she had wanted few things in her life. "One kiss," she agreed on a sigh that was so soft, so yielding that she didn't recognize her own voice.

But Killian did. It was the voice he had heard in his dreams, the voice that made a mockery of the woman he had thought her to be. He took her lips lightly, gently, teasing instead of capturing, inviting instead of plundering. His need for her body was white hot, but his consideration for her mind, her emotions was more caring.

Silke gave herself to his kiss, expecting passion and getting that elusive fantasy called tenderness. Delicate as the dawn, it breached her defenses simply by slipping through them as though they didn't exist. His warmth called to her. She cuddled closer, her head pillowed on his shoulder as he explored her mouth with almost lazy thoroughness. When he finally lifted his head, she was somehow sitting in his lap, cradled in his arms. She felt the child she had never had a chance to be and a woman unlike any lie had been to date. She studied his face, the deep glow in his dark eyes, unable to look away, not wanting even words to destroy the silence of this one moment in time. She reached up, her fingers tracing his jaw, copying the first caress he had given her. His mouth was next to claim—the lips that had given her pleasure so drugging that she wanted more.

"I like your idea of being friends," Killian murmured huskily. "I've never had a friend like you."

"Neither have I," she whispered, forgetting what she was supposed to be, remembering only what she was when he held her.

Killian searched her eyes, seeing the truth, accepting it as he wouldn't have days before. Whatever she had shared with other men, it had never been this. They were magic together, and in this they were both virgins. As he bent his head to take her lips once more, he found the idea good, satisfying, and more special than anything he had claimed as his own in years.

"Killian, both of us together will never eat all of that," Silke protested, staring at the vegetables he was putting in the grocery cart.

"I like vegetables and you said you could cook. I thought, since we're friends, you wouldn't mind taking pity on me." He dropped a plastic bag of handpicked onions on top of the pile, then started on the potatoes.

Silke followed along behind, hardly noticing that, for a man who didn't cook, he was very picky about what went into the cart. "You want me to cook for you?"

"Sort of." He cast a quick look over his shoulder, seeing nothing in Silke's expression to indicate she was digging in her heels. "I had in mind a kind of tradeoff. I'd drive us to work, and you would teach me the basics. We'd both win. I wouldn't starve and you won't have to cut into your limited budget with the expense of gas."

Silke frowned, considering the idea. Her first reaction was acceptance, although she had no intentions of telling Killian that. "I don't think this kind of thing is exactly what my parents had in mind for this year," she said finally, referring to her mother's plan, which she had seen no reason to hide.

He shrugged and wandered down the frozen food aisle. "You said the only rules were that you had to live on your three thousand until you got a job and a place to live. You were supposed to make friends who didn't trade on your name or influence, and you were supposed to do something useful with yourself. As far as I can see, you would be doing all of that."

Put like that, Silke had to admit it sounded as though she was following the guidelines set down by her parents.

"It doesn't have to be a permanent thing unless we both want it that way," Killian added persuasively, joining her at the cart.

"All right. But I think I'm getting the best of the deal."

He grinned, bent, and gave her a kiss before she could realize what he intended. "Don't you believe it. You haven't seen me in the kitchen."

Six

"That's the last of the dishes," Silke announced as she closed the cabinet.

Killian took the damp dish towel from her hand and tossed it on the clean counter behind them. "It's almost dawn. Tired now?"

She nodded. "Another hour or so and I'll be able to sleep."

"Then we have time to try some of that cocoa before you go."

She shook her head. "No. You're beat." She covered his mouth with her hand before he could object. "You are. I can see it. My sleeping habits are my problem and I'm used to dealing with them."

He circled her wrist, placing a kiss in the center of her palm before he pulled her hand away. "This morning it is our problem." He pulled out one of his new saucepans, filled it with water, and put it on to boil. "Besides, hasn't it occurred to you that I just might not want to let you go just yet? I'm enjoying the first night we have spent together. I've never been to an all-night market in my life. I had no idea there were that many people who did their shopping that late. Come to think of it, I also have never paid any attention to how much stuff the modern grocery store carries." He opened a cabinet and pulled out the box of cocoa mix, frowning mildly at the marshmallows advertised on the front. "I still think plain would have been fine."

Silke laughed and gave in. She was learning that Killian was the proverbial immovable object when he got an idea in his head. "I like marshmallows," she said, as she reached for two cups.

The humor in his eyes approved her decision to stay.

"Just don't think because I'm letting you bully me into staying for a little longer that you'll always get your way." She set the cups on the counter beside the stove.

"Do I look that dumb?"

"No, just that stubborn."

"Not nice, sexy lady."

"The water's boiling."

Killian didn't even glance at the pot. "I can't cook, remember?"

"Boiling water isn't cooking."

"No, but making hot chocolate is."

"I give up," Silke muttered.

Killian caught her close, ignoring her gasp of surprise. "How much do you give up?"

"Not that much." She braced her hands against his chest, trying to look serious when all she wanted to do was laugh.

"You know you enjoy it."

Silke sobered, her body tensing in his grasp. "Don't spoil it, Killian. I like you. Don't make me regret letting you in. Don't bring up what you think I am."

Killian froze. The last things he had been thinking about were her past, her reputation, or his assignment. "I didn't mean it like that," he said honestly.

She studied him intently, the steady way he held her eyes. "You're sure?"

He nodded. "I'm not lily-white either. I don't think I would want to be even if I could be. I remember what it felt like when I finally got a long, hard look at reality. Hell with no escape. It wasn't, of course. There is heaven mixed in, too. But I had to lose my damn innocence to know that."

Something dark and cold moved inside of Silke, hairline cracks letting in slivers of light, of warmth. She stirred in his arms, frightened suddenly as she hadn't been in years. She had thought she understood herself too well to be surprised anymore. Held close to this man's heart, she discovered her error. Need. A simple, four-letter word. A terrible complication, a trap, a prison.

"Don't do this, Killian," she whispered, her lashes dropping to hide the unexpected welling of tears in her eyes. One drop spilled over, a crystal of grief to freeze on her cheek.

"Do what, Silke?" Killian stroked the moisture away, his face tight with the demands he was making on his body. He wanted to take her, lock them both in a world of passion so neither could remember the present. For the first time in his life, illusion seemed safer than truth. "Talk to me. Don't shut me out."

"I can't."

"You won't."

She opened her eyes then, her lashes starred with tears. "Both. I don't know you."

He shook his head. "You do. Your body certainly does. Do you think I didn't watch you deliberately ignoring me that first time? Do you think I don't feel every wall you build between us? Do you think I don't know that even now, with your body screaming for mine, you won't walk right out that door, denying us both for some reason I don't understand? I'm hurting you. I can feel that, too. Help me to stop. Help me to understand, because as sure as I'm standing here, I'm not leaving you. You can run, although I don't think you will. You can fight, and that I am definitely sure you will do. But you won't win. I can't let you." He cupped her face in his palms, staring into her eyes, willing her to trust him. "Open your door, Silke. Let me in."

Silke swayed closer, her physical need growing so strong that she couldn't hold back. She lifted her mouth, wanting his lips, wanting to forget the past and knowing it had never been closer, more alive.

Killian stared at her lips, his blind desire blotting out thought. The power of his own arousal tore at his restraint. "No, Silke. No matter what you have done before, I won't go the way of our senses, damn you." He shook her once. "Look at me." He waited for her eyes to open. "As I breathe, I want you in my bed. But I want your mind first, virgin territory, unclaimed, held separate, safe. You won't lay with me and hold yourself back. I am not a few hours of pleasure, and I won't let you be either."

Cold crept over her, rejection, fear. Memories, damning, dark and deep. Hands that had held released. Bodies that had yielded stiffened. "Let me go."

"Afraid?" he challenged her.

"Yes."

Shocked, Killian looked deeper. "Of me?" he demanded with sudden harshness.

"Myself." She pushed against his chest, twisting when he wouldn't let her go. "You have no right."

"I'm taking it anyway."

"Then I'll fight." Her head thrown back, her red hair tongues of fire, her golden eyes icy shards of temper.

"Then you're a fool." He stroked her breast gently, caressing the soft mound. "You might win against me but not against both of us." He teased the nipple that was already hard and wanting. "I don't want you defeated."

Angry, Silke jerked away, this time escaping because he let her go. "No, you want surrender." If he had been angry, she could have handled that. Instead, she saw compassion in his eyes, tenderness and the faintest overlay of pity. The last did what all that had gone before did not. With an oath that had its roots in her days on the street, she swung on her heel and headed for the door.

Killian let her reach for the knob before he spoke. "You will come to me, Silke. But not in surrender. I want no broken adversary for my woman. I want your strength, your cunning, your clever mind and the agony of those memories you keep locked so tightly away. You will give me those because you want to, not because you can't help yourself any longer."

"I will give you nothing," she said roughly as she yanked open the door. She nearly screamed when he caught her shoulders, turning her before she could escape.

"You have already given me something." He smiled at her hiss of rage. Sliding his fingers through her hair, he held her head still as he touched his lips to her forehead. "One day I'll tell you what it is." He released her and stepped back, grinning at the shock, the confusion that crowded out the fury in her eyes. "Do you need any help slamming the door in my face?"

"Hell no," she shouted, whirling away and crashing the panel for all she was worth. His chuckle was the last straw to her sorely tried temper. For every step she took, she had a graphic curse or aspersion to cast on his ancestry or manhood. When she reached her own bare apartment, she all but ripped the clothes from her body and flung herself into his sleeping bag. Immediately, his scent enfolded her. If she had been a cat, she would have been spitting with rage. She scrambled out of the bag, kicked it for good measure, stalked the bedroom, glaring at the offending pallet. The floor was hard. She was tired. She was also nuts. So what if it smelled like him? She'd be sleeping. She'd never notice. Screwy reasoning, but so what? She crawled back into the bag, practically holding her breath as she snuggled down.

"The first thing in the morning, I'm getting a bed," she muttered as she closed her eyes.

In seconds she slept. The night still lay curled around the city but she didn't know it. The nightmares didn't come. Only Killian's image lay in her thoughts, teasing her body, tantalizing her mind, bringing alive dreams she had never known. The tension in her face eased. Her lips softened, curving up into a smile that would have intrigued Killian had he been there to see. She sighed delicately, turning in his bed, reaching for the feel of him, to match the scent of him that still lingered to embrace her. Dawn peeked across the sky and still she slept, deeply, soundly for the first time in years. And when the thunder rumbled, she only turned from the sound. But it grew stronger, more demanding, until she opened one eye. The sky outside the window was clear. It wasn't raining. No rain. No thunder. She frowned, opening the other eye. Knocking. She groaned, muttering to herself, and crawled out of the sleeping bag.

"All right. All right. I'm coming." She stumbled to her case, still lying on the floor. "Where is that robe?" Finally, she found the swathe of yellow and pulled it on. She reached the door, still groping for the belt that wasn't there.

"Open the door, Silke. It's time to get up."

"I might have known," she mumbled, holding the robe together with one hand as she unlocked the door with the other.

Killian stared at her, the tousled hair, the sleepy eyes, and the soft flush of slumber that lay on her skin. "It's almost ten," he said, leaning down to brush her lips before he eased past her into the apartment. "I thought we could have breakfast before we go. But I can help you shower and dress if you would rather."

"You could also be helping yourself into a pine box," she warned irritably, wishing she didn't like the taste of his mouth so much. She could still feel his kiss, the touch of his body on hers. The urge to walk into his arms and receive a real good-morning caress was so real that she took a step toward him.

Killian saw the change in her eyes. He stilled, waiting, knowing it was too soon, but tempted nonetheless to take what he could get. The night had been too long. "Do it, Silke," he encouraged deeply.

She took another step. One more and she would be there. She froze, shaking her head. "I won't let you do this to me."

"Still fighting." He grinned, tucked his hands in his pockets, and gave her a wink. "All right. I can wait. I rather like dreaming about you."

"You, too?" Silke said before she thought, then groaned in disgust at his pleased expression.

"That settles it." He stole the last foot between them, wrapped her in his arms, and shared the kiss that they both wanted.

Her mouth opened at the first touch of his, hot and needing. He took her, letting her feel just what his dreams had been like. His hands stroked over her, sliding over the satin robe, molding it to her. When she moaned softly, he pressed into the small of her back, tipping her hips up into the cradle of his thighs. She was heaven in his arms. Woman yielding and taking with equal strength. When he lifted his head, he was breathing deeply, her scent filling him as he wished he could fill her.

Silke opened her eyes to look straight into his. No smile lay there for her to latch on to. No simple emotion gave her an escape. This man meant to claim her. He was serious, asking things of her that no one had ever known lived within her. Suddenly she had questions of her own. But was she brave enough to ask them?

"No protest, Silke?" Killian murmured, studying her intently. There was something new this morning. She was thinking instead of reacting.

"No. I wanted you to kiss me."

"And?"

"I want to know why. A man intent on an affair wouldn't care what was in my head."

"I never said I wanted an affair."

"How could you want anything else?"

"Your reputation?"

She looked away from his probing eyes. "Yes."

He caught her chin, turning her to face him once more. "It matters. I'd be lying if I said it didn't. But I am not judging you now. I'm asking."

"And if I tell you I earned it, willfully, knowing what I did even as I was doing it?"

"I'd want to know why," he replied flatly, his hands tightening on her hip, her chin. "Up until four years ago, you led a relatively gossip-free-life. Then suddenly you went wild. The newspapers were full of your escapades. The crowd you ran with were some of the worst in your group."

"You sound like an investigator or a reporter."

"I am an investigator."

She stared at him, stunned at the casual way he threw out the information.

"That's what I'll be talking to my friend about this morning. With any luck I'll be head of his security before the day is over," he added blandly as he released her and stepped back.

"You're serious, aren't you?"

He inclined his head. He glanced at his watch. "You'd better get ready or neither one of us will end up with a job today."

"But . . ." Silke protested.

Killian turned her in the direction of her bedroom. "Go take your shower. I can't cook much, but I can manage oven toast and coffee. It will be waiting for you when you're done." He tapped her lightly on the bottom.

She glared at him over her shoulder but did as ordered, showering quickly and selecting the outfit from the limited number of clothes she had brought with her. For every question she got answered, Killian created others more demanding. She didn't understand him. Or herself, she admitted silently as she finished putting on her makeup.

"Hurry up, Silke," Killian called from the kitchen.

"I'm coming," she muttered, grabbing her handbag and stalking through the empty living room.

Killian ran an appreciative eye over the tailored pink suit and white jabot blouse that added a feminine touch. "Good enough to eat," he murmured with a grin.

She picked up a piece of toast still warm from the oven and nibbled at it. "Just so it's good enough to get hired."

"Just smile at Mickey, sexy lady, and you'll be home free."

Silke's brows rose at the mention of Maggie's husband's name. "How do you know him?"

"I told you his brother and I are friends. Did you think I lied?" He looked at her, his brows set at a sharp angle of inquiry.

"No. You don't seem to be a man who would bother with a lie."

Relaxing, he leaned forward, kissing her on the forehead. "Thanks, beautiful Silke."

The warmth was there again, seductive, addictive. She couldn't fight what she didn't understand. "Why do you do that?"

"Do what?"

"Kiss me like that?"

He didn't say anything for a moment as he considered his words. So much had changed since he had met this woman. "It pleases me," he said finally, honestly.

"How can it?"

He smiled faintly at her surprise, sharing it even if he didn't intend admitting it. "You mean because it isn't your mouth I'm taking?"

She nodded without looking away. She felt strange when Killian touched her like that. Small, fragile, and all woman. Protected without being diminished by that protection.

"It's called affection, Silke, not sex, not passion, just simple liking for the person you are." As he said the words, he realized that he meant every one. No matter what Silke had been or would be, he liked her. She was vulnerable, which he hadn't expected, funny, tender when she wasn't flashing those wicked eyes at him, daring him to do his damnedest, and most of all, surprised by things that he had taken for granted for years. Despite the veneer of toughness that was as much a part of her as her tawny eyes, there was an underlying aura of innocence that demanded care and delicate handling.

"You like me?" Liking had always seemed such a trivial thing in her life that she didn't think about it at all, especially in regard to herself.

"Yes, much to my surprise."

The warmth that had begun to grow in her died. "My reputation," she stated flatly, hurt when she least expected it.

Killian caught the flash of pain in her expression, silently damning his candor but unable to call it back. Instead he reached out, stroking her cheek. He had made himself some promises in the early hours of the morning. He would give Silke as much truth as possible and still protect her. One day she would have to know why he had come to Atlanta. He couldn't change that, but he didn't have to add a list of lies to the tally.

"You're here now. You said you intended to change. Stop tearing yourself up for what was. All of us, myself included, can only move on when each page of life is turned. To hold on to one piece is to stop the progression of the story, the evolution."

"Do you think it's possible for anyone to make this kind of change?" she asked bitterly.

"I've lived too long not to believe that even miracles are possible if the will and the wanting are strong enough. I think we both have enough of each." He traced her lips with his forefinger. "Now, smile for me. Today is your first day of your new life. And mine. That should be cause for celebration."

Silke wished, for one fleeting moment, that she was the kind to run when the way turned crooked and bumpy. But she wasn't. She fought, sometimes too long and with no chance of winning.

Maybe the odds weren't in her favor here. Maybe she couldn't undo or smooth over her past. But she had to try. She stared into Killian's blue eyes and found something she hadn't had even with her family, someone to test her, to dare her to give the best of herself. It was a strange feeling—a demand and a plea. The first stiffened her backbone, the second drew her closer, her lips softening. She kissed the tip of his finger as it made its last sweep, her eyes glowing with tenderness that she was learning from him. Her lips curved gently and her smile became his.

"A new beginning," she whispered.

Seven

"You wanted to see me, Hollander?" Ricky said, dropping wearily into the single chair facing his boss's desk.

"It took you long enough to get here," Hollander growled, stuffing his chewed-off cigar, unlit, into his mouth. He had given up smoking two years before and his disposition still hadn't recovered. "You sure Silke got off all right?"

"Yeah. I watched her get on the plane myself." Ricky frowned. "That guy I told you about got on with her. Didn't seem to be paying any attention, but then he wouldn't have if he was sent to get rid of her." He yanked a snapshot out of his pocket and tossed it on Hollander's desk. "I got this of him. I was just on my way to have it checked out when I got your message."

Hollander glared down at the photograph, chomping on his pacifier. He frowned heavily, his lined face getting even more marks with the expression. "Damn it to hell. I know him. That's Killian Carpenter. What the hell is he doing following her?"

"I didn't say he was for sure." Ricky sat up straighter. "Who is that guy? I don't know the name."

"You wouldn't since you haven't been here all that long." He looked up to glare at Ricky. "That's the problem with imported talent."

"I wish you'd get off my case about my being here. You know

damn well you were running out of narcs you could rope in who weren't already known around here." He glared right back at Hollander. "I ripped up my life, in case you're interested, to come to Philly."

Hollander sighed deeply, slumping back in his chair. "All right. Stop breathing fire. It isn't good for my digestion."

Ricky relaxed. "So who is Killian? And why are you so sure he's following Silke?"

"I'm sure because that's what the man does, among other things very similar, or to be more specific, that's what his company does. I know damn well you have to have heard of Carpenter Inc."

Ricky's brows rose in surprise. "He's *that* Carpenter?"

"Yeah. And he's also a friend of the St. Jameses. Does their security work for them."

"You think they hired him to keep an eye on Silke?"

"It makes sense up to a point. If all the St. Jameses were worried about was their little lamb . . ." He ignored Ricky's snort at his description of Silke. ". . . the tail would just be one of Killian's men, not the man himself."

Ricky swore softly, fluently.

"Not bad, kid."

Ricky ignored the name Hollander had been calling him since the beginning. "How do they know what she's been doing? I would bet anything that I own that Silke kept her word about not telling her family."

"I hate amateurs," Hollander grunted angrily. "That crazy woman could blow this whole deal."

"How? She isn't here."

"If you spotted Killian, what's to say some other imbecile hasn't done the same thing? We both know that our quarry is suspicious. You can't be sure you were the only one following Silke to make sure she got out of town."

"So what do we do?"

"I don't know." Hollander poked his fingers through what little hair he had and glowered at Ricky. "I damn well don't want to inform the St. Jameses, especially if they *don't* know. I'd like to keep my job long enough to retire with a full pension."

"Wouldn't we all," Ricky agreed with feeling.

"But we can't leave her out there either. The St. Jameses will hang our rumps out to dry if something happens to that crazy woman."

"One of us could contact Killian. Put him in the picture."

"From his mouth to Geoffrey St. James's ear."

"Then you think of something," Ricky shot back.

"It would be nice if you remembered who's the boss around here," Hollander retaliated.

Ricky glared, then muttered an apology.

"I think I'll give the chief in Atlanta a call, put him on alert."

"That's it?"

"For now. Just, for all our sakes, keep your ears open. If there is any move made on Silke St. James, I want to know before it goes down. Then we'll scream bloody murder, wrap her in cotton batting if we have to."

"You want me to do what?" Spike Douglas asked, staring at Killian.

Killian grinned at his friend's dumbfounded expression. It sat uneasily on the thin, aristocratic features, barely shielded by narrow, dark-rimmed glasses. In spite of his nickname, Spike was a financial wiz of the first order. "I want you to employ me as your head of security. For a year. For the salary . . ."

"Of one dollar," Spike finished irritably. "I know. I heard you the first time. I'm just having trouble handling the image of you as my employee. As anyone's employee," he added when Killian chuckled.

"You don't think I can take orders?"

"I know you can't," Spike muttered bluntly.

"Well, I'll take yours."

"Why?"

"A client. I'm keeping an eye on a woman who is, right now, downstairs with your brother applying for a job as a receptionist."

"And?"

"What and? I'm telling you the whole thing."

"Not likely. You don't take a year off from your company to follow some little receptionist around. You gave up fieldwork a long time ago. So give."

"I may have given it up, but it didn't give me up. There was an outbreak of summer flu. We're shorthanded."

"Still doesn't wash, Kill. What's the rest?"

"How does Silke Brown-St. James sound?"

Spike's eyes narrowed. "The only one by that name I have ever heard of was one of the adopted daughters of the St. Jameses of Philly."

"Got it in one."

"What the devil does she want with a job as my receptionist?"

"If I tell you, it can't go any farther than here."

"You know you don't have to say that."

Killian inclined his head before he proceeded to outline the situation to date. By the time he finished, any hint of humor or relaxation had deserted Spike.

"Just how dangerous do you think this stalker is? And did he follow her? Because I can tell you right now, I don't need any more problems. This expansion thing is enough of a headache as it is."

"I don't know to the first, and as far as the second, he hasn't shown up here. But that doesn't mean he won't," he admitted. "Silke's going wasn't a secret by any means."

"Damn," Spike swore, then shifted in his chair. He glared at Killian. "I don't know why I always let you talk me into these things."

"Think of what you'll be getting out of the deal. I'm good even if I do say so myself."

"Good enough to make up for a femme fatale socialite at my switchboard?" Spike demanded.

"It won't be that bad. If Silke tries something, she does it well."

"I thought you said you didn't know her," Spike said suspiciously.

"Not in the way you mean, I don't. But I have studied her."

"And you like her," Spike observed in surprise.

Killian inclined his head. "I do."

"That reputation of hers would choke a horse."

"Neither one of us is lily white either."

Spike scowled, then grinned when Killian just looked at him. "There is that. Still doesn't seem right."

"Right hasn't got much to do with this job."

Spike considered the options, then nodded. "All right. I'll take you and her on. But if I end up with a mess down here, you will never hear the end of it." He rose to his full height of five feet eleven. "And that's a promise."

Killian got to his feet, not even noticing the difference of a few inches. Spike was a giant by anyone's measure. "Don't worry so much. I could be charging you a consulting fee."

"Don't push it, Kill," Spike advised, walking into the hall.

Killian laughed as he followed his friend. One more place had been added to the circle of protection he was slowly weaving around Silke.

"I hate this thing," Silke muttered, glaring at the form with all its blank lines. She was alone in the room of narrow tables and plastic chairs. Mickey had been apologetic about the lack of appointments, explaining that the office furniture that had been ordered had been delayed. Silke filled in a few more facts, chewing on the end of the pen between answers. All this work for one insignificant job of answering phones and smiling at the right moment. "It's a wonder they don't want to know my bra size."

"I would," Killian murmured, leaning over to stare at the half completed application.

Silke tipped back her head, glaring at him. "What are you doing here? Didn't get the job?"

"I got it. And I finished my appointment a few minutes ago."

"I don't want to hear this. Besides, smugness is not an attractive trait."

He laughed softly and kissed the tip of her nose before she could pull away. "Stop frowning. You'll ruin that gorgeous face." He cupped her head, turning her so that she had to look at the form. "Get busy, and when you finish, we'll blow this place. I'm starving. And we still have to hit the utility companies and the furniture places." He settled his chin on her hair, his hands braced on her shoulders.

Silke wanted to lean back, yield to his strength. Instead, she glared at the paper in front of her. "Will you behave before someone comes in and sees you draped all over me?"

"But I like being draped all over you." Even as he objected, he moved back to give her room. One hand stayed on her shoulder, a link between them in a way he didn't want to admit.

Silke hesitated, liking the feel of him touching her. She hadn't realized until this second how carefully she had been tuned to his return. Suddenly the paperwork didn't seem so irritating after all. Her pen zipped across bare lines, filling in the edited facts of her life. "Done," she announced a few moments later.

Killian slipped the paper out of her hands, scanned it quickly, then nodded. "I'll turn this in to Mickey while you do whatever women do and then we'll find a place to eat."

Silke rose, grabbed her handbag, smiling at his one-track mind. In some ways she felt as though she had known Killian for years. There was an ease about being with him that had never been present with any other man. He made her feel cherished. An old-fashioned word when she hadn't thought she was capable of feeling old-fashioned values and beliefs. She was still smiling over her own strange behavior as she rejoined Killian in the lobby of Douglas Plastics.

"When we get somewhere private, you will have to tell me what that look is about," Killian said as he tucked her into the front seat of his car.

"For my ears only," she replied as he slid into the seat beside her.

"Then I'll guess."

She laughed, leaning back to enjoy the ride. "You can try," she invited.

He slanted her a look. "You have the most wicked smile I have ever seen."

"Good. I never liked being one of a crowd."

"I don't think you could be that if you tried."

"Compliments, compliments." She tossed her head, then leaned across and brushed her lips over his cheek.

Killian jerked, not having expected the caress. So far in their relationship, he had done all the pursuing. Having the tables turned was unnerving. "Damn it, woman. The least you could have done was wait until I didn't have my hands full with this traffic."

Silke's amusement was a slow, seductive ripple of delight at her own happiness and his reaction to her. "I think I'm going to like this new life stuff."

"What is it, my dear?" Geoffrey asked gently as he watched his wife pace the breakfast room. "I would think you would be pleased after Killian's call. Silke has settled in nicely. She has an apartment and a job with Killian's friend."

"I can't get this drug business out of my mind. Maybe you were right. Maybe we should have told Killian the whole story. If anything happens to Silke, I will never forgive myself." She came to Geoffrey, taking the hands he held out and sitting down beside him. "Maybe we should call him."

Geoffrey didn't try to placate Lorraine with assurances that were little more than useless words. He was worried, too. "Before we do that, I was thinking it might be a better idea to talk to the man who was Silke's boss. We could find out if they consider her to be in danger. There is no sense in alerting Killian to a threat that might not even exist."

"We don't know who her boss was."

Geoffrey's eyes hardened, narrowing with determination. "I will find out."

"Will that be dangerous for Silke?"

"I shouldn't think so. The commissioner is a friend. He can get the information without anyone but the two of us knowing about it."

"I feel so helpless."

"Killian will look after her."

The room was opulent, richly appointed without being flamboyant. There was a feel of timelessness about it and the house and grounds around it. Although new money had bought the estate and many of the servants, no one would have guessed it by walking the corridors and rooms. Teas were held here, charity events, business and social gatherings for some of Philadelphia's elite. A life that many dream of went on behind the ironwork gates. But there was a darker side to the soft life, shadows cast by a villain disguised as a philanthropic businessman.

James Spano made his money on the streets, in the alleys, in the back rooms of dirty little crack houses that changed locations in the wee hours of the morning. He held the city in the palm of his hand, and the funny thing was, most of the inhabitants didn't even know they were under siege. Oh, they knew of the drugs in the streets, in the schools. It gave them something to complain and lament about when politics and sports became a bore. The decay and crime drugs brought made good cocktail conversation. James, "Jimmy," had even participated in those discussions, his comments just as blasé, narrow, and useless as all the rest of the rhetoric. Meanwhile, he raked in his thousands per hour from a network that covered most of eastern Pennsylvania. Today, however, he was far from blasé. Someone was rocking his particular yacht on the sea of human greed. The ground swell was rising and the storm approaching with more speed than even he could have anticipated.

"Did you find out where the leak was coming from?" he demanded, his voice menacingly soft.

The thin, nervous man in front of him nodded. "I think so."

"You think?" Slender brows punctuated the sarcasm in his tone.

The other man flushed, shifting in his chair. "We think it was a woman named Silke St. James."

Jimmy frowned, startled at the identity of his nemesis. "And how did you arrive at this conclusion?"

"One of our mules got picked up a couple of weeks ago. While she was being booked, she happened to see a man that she knew. Turns out he was a narc. It also turns out that for a while last year this narc was engaged to this St. James woman and ran with the rich crowd."

"And?"

"I started looking around, asking questions. Knew you wanted the leak bad."

"And you knew I'd pay for the information."

The man nodded again. "You've always been fair."

"And I will be in this . . ." He held up a hand when the man would have interrupted. ". . . but only if it checks out."

"But I did all of that. She's it I tell you."

"Then you have nothing to worry about. You'll get your money when I'm satisfied and not before."

The man bit his lips, the urge to argue just marginally less than his instinct for survival. "All right," he agreed sullenly.

Jimmy waved him to the door. "I'll get in touch with you when I want to see you again."

The moment he was alone, Jimmy picked up the phone to dial his contact in the law enforcement community. Thirty minutes later he hung up, his face rigid with fury barely contained. "You're dead, Silke St. James," he whispered darkly. "Dead and you don't even know it yet. Nobody messes with Jimmy Spano."

Eight

"Well, what do you think?" Silke demanded, standing back to inspect her new bed. The white comforter and eyelet sheets invited sleep and went well with the teal blue carpet in the bedroom.

"It looks almost as good as mine. And a lot better than the sleeping bags we used last night," Killian replied, wrapping his arms around her waist and drawing her back against him. "But I figured we'd both be sleeping on the floor again tonight. I never realized what a potent weapon a woman's lashes and a sexy, I-need-your-help voice could be. You had that salesman ready to bring our beds in on his back if he had to."

Silke tipped her head up so that she could see his face. "You didn't seem to mind."

"I don't. I knew you were playing one of your games." He turned her in his arms, liking her when she looked at him with those golden eyes full of questions, tiny doubts that demanded his reassurance. Her softness was always so surprising, so seductively enticing. "But I would mind very much if you played for real."

She searched his gaze, seeing the truth written clearly in the blue depths. The certainty in the first part of his statement startled her, but the possessiveness of the last made her uneasy. She'd have to address his feelings and her own soon. But not now, not when night was creeping ever closer, not when she wanted this ease they had established to stay, to hold the fear at bay. So instead, she tackled the knowledge he seemed to have of her. "How did you know I wasn't serious?"

Killian studied her face, the features that showed so little sometimes and far too much others. "I can't give you tangibles. I just know. Just like I knew that Ricky person who held you in the garden that night wasn't reaching you. Nor was anyone else there. You give yourself up to a point, then you stand back, untouched. At first I thought you were a tease, the kind of woman who likes to have men dangling from a string yanked by passion never fulfilled but always implied. I had to see you in action twice before I realized that, whatever was driving you, that wasn't it."

She frowned at the assessment. She had thought her skill detection-proof. It should have been, considering her practice. She looked beyond Killian, considering the ramifications of his discovery. If anyone else had his sight, she had left those who had trod this path with her in danger. She shivered, knowing too well just the kind of punishment that would be meted out.

Killian felt her shiver and drew her closer, frowning at the reaction he hadn't expected. Fear lay in her eyes, changing the gold to hammered yellow. There was tension now where there had been only softness. "You have that look again," he murmured, cupping her cheek, demanding that she focus on him instead of some distant point he could not see. "Don't pull away from me. I won't hurt you. You don't need to stand back from me." He stroked the lines of worry marring her brow. "I will help you with anything. All you have to do is tell me."

Such a simple gift, so seldom offered in her life. "You shouldn't make blanket promises like that. I might try to take you up on them," she replied, trying for a light touch.

Killian tensed, angered at her tone. "It won't work, Silke."

His challenge. Should she accept or play the game? Maybe lose? His look demanded honesty. He had even promised her the truth. Did he deserve evasions and lies in return? Hard choices. A turning point leading down a road she had never traveled. She was afraid, of what he could make her feel, of the past that would tear apart her future, of the present that could very well be harboring the shadow of death.

"Run or play, sexy lady?" Killian demanded.

Silke lifted her head, her hair of flame a banner of her own spirit. "Play. My rules."

He smiled, more relieved than he intended to allow her to see. With this woman he didn't dare show any weakness. Something in her past had taught her how to survive by finding the soft spot and using it for her own protection. "Until I find I don't like them."

She laughed, relaxing against him again. "Don't be so sure of yourself."

"I could warn you of the same thing."

"Arrogance."

He didn't deny it. Rather he turned it to his advantage. "We both have it."

"A gentleman wouldn't have said that."

"I never said I was a gentleman."

He bent his head, taking her lips, needing her taste to celebrate the step closer he had just gained. He expected resistance but received compliance, her mouth fusing with his, as eager for his touch as he for hers. Her hands slid through his hair, holding him, claiming him. His fingers tightened on her hips, tipping her until she pressed against the need growing ever more demanding. As he raised his head, he studied her flushed face, the sultry eyes that made no secret of the passion he had brought to life. The bed could have been miles away for all the attention he paid to it.

"You may kill us if you don't stop holding back," he whispered roughly.

"I'm not holding back," she answered huskily, rotating her hips just enough to deepen the mating of their bodies. "I want you as I have never wanted any other man." She had never spoken of need to another soul. Her life had taught her the folly of ever being that vulnerable. But with this man, the rules she had made were no longer so inviolate.

He was tempted. His hands curled into her soft flesh, unknowingly marking her. Her scent was a silent tease to his senses. Every breath he drew was filled with her. Her heat was stealing his control, the feel of her hands on him pure pleasure that he was a fool to deny. His jaw rigid with the force of his decision, he stepped back. He saw the shock in her eyes, the confusion that had been there before, the hurt.

"I told you I wouldn't take you like this. You are not a body to me. You never wanted to be one of a crowd. Well, neither do I. You will not give me what you have given others. I want more. I will have more or I will have nothing." Each word was harsher than the last, more telling of the strength of will that had chosen this almost impossible course.

"You ask too much," she retaliated.

"And you have always asked too little," he snapped angrily, separating them completely. He rammed his hands in his pockets to keep from reaching out to her. He could feel her pain as his own.

If he had slapped her, he could not have hurt her more. Silke's face paled, her eyes cat yellow as she poised to defend herself. "So I am cheap now."

"Not in my eyes. Your own."

Her hand raised, the nails claws to wound. Killian didn't even flinch as the strike came. The blow never landed. Silke raked her fingers to one side, missing his cheek. The air whispered angrily at the power lost in the aborted contact.

"Damn you," she gasped, her breath coming in pants of anger and frustration with no relief in sight. "Get out of here. Don't come back."

Killian moved toward the door. "I'm going. But not for good. You couldn't hurt me then. Think about that, Silke. Another man would have felt the slash of your hand, but you couldn't do it to me."

"Reflex," she said scornfully, eyes flashing pure rage.

He glanced over his shoulder, his expression compassionate and even a little weary. "If you ever had those kinds of reflexes, you've trained them out of yourself. I've never seen you make a move that you didn't intend. And I don't know another woman who could have stopped herself as you just did."

For an instant their eyes met. Silke stilled, held by a power as strong and as focused as her own. Had Killian poured icy water on the fire of her temper he couldn't have doused it so completely with just that one soul-deep look. He was a mirror of herself she didn't want to see.

"Just think. Look for what you don't see. I had to," he murmured softly before walking away.

Silke listened to her apartment door close gently. The silence
folded around her—empty, colorless, cold. "I can't," she whispered. "It's taken me too long to put the pieces back together
again."

Tears filled her eyes, drifting over her lashes, sliding delicately
down her cheeks. Had she wept with wild fury, had she thrown
herself into the pain and let it win the battle of her will, perhaps
relief would have come. Instead, she dammed the flow to this
slow trickle of grief and defeat where no ease or comfort was
offered or found. She cooked her dinner and ate it without caring
what she did. She showered and chose her clothes for the following day with the same kind of listlessness. And when she turned
out the lights at midnight and crawled into her new bed, she faced
the blackness of the night with nothing to hold on to, not even
her own belief in herself. As she lay in the inky silence, the memories came, the sounds of strangers in her home, the laughter that
held no amusement, the moans of lust, the smell of liquor. Her
eyes widened as her hands clenched the new sheets into a crum-
pled mass of white. She tried to push the images away, but still
they came, growing, demanding she feel the terror of the child
she had been then, helpless, frightened beyond words to tell, and
at the mercy of a hostile environment filled with eyes that knew
none of the softness, the good of life.

Shaking, she stumbled out of bed, going to the kitchen for a
drink of water that didn't help. The nightmares followed. She
paced. They chased. She hugged her arms around her middle and
still felt the icy fingers of that child's fate slide ever closer. Leaning her head against the kitchen wall, she moaned deeply, silently
begging for amnesia.

Killian leaned his back against the wall as he sat on the car-
peted floor, his legs stretched out in front of him, and nursed his
brandy. He who was rarely lonely was missing one female who
spelled nothing but trouble. He hadn't meant to upset her, but
Silke had a way of blowing every plan he had ever made right
out of the water. He shook his head and took another sip of his

drink. He had raised his glass for another drink when his hand stilled. The faint moan at his back came again, louder this time more distressed.

"Silke!" He rose in one fluid motion and was out of the apartment in three strides, every sense alert to danger. Using the extra key that she didn't know he had, he unlocked her door, and eased into the darkness, his stocking feet making no sound to destroy the silence. Another moan led him to the kitchen. His eyes, already adjusted to the darkness lit only by the moonlight filtered through the drapes in the living room, picked out Silke's huddled shape against the far wall. He glanced around quickly, assuring himself that there was no intruder. Then he went to her, taking her in his arms.

Silke jerked at his touch, stiffening, her head coming up like a frightened animal's. The silver light caught the tortured expression on her face, the glazed look of terror before she could disguise it. Killian inhaled sharply, his hold tightening as he lifted her fully into his arms and carried her toward the bedroom.

"Don't take me back there. I can't bear it," she protested brokenly.

"It's the only damn furniture you've got," he replied roughly. "And you won't be alone this time. I'm not leaving." He went down on his knees to place her in the middle of the bed, then he made a place for himself beside her.

Escape her only thought, Silke tried to scramble away. She was too vulnerable. She couldn't let him see what she felt. It was bad enough she had to know. Killian wrapped an arm around her waist and chained her to his length, his body heat a brand through the thin satin of her nightgown. Silke fought him like a wild thing, all arms and legs and bucking body. Killian grunted irritably when he lost a battle or two with a limb until he finally had her pinned with a leg across her thighs and her arms stretched above her head, her wrists locked together in a manacle of one of his hands.

"Enough, Silke," he commanded, turning her face so that she had to look at him.

"Get off me." Panic that had its roots in her memory and in the feel of his body against hers sharpened her voice.

Killian heard the panic. With another woman he would have taken a different route. But Silke demanded more than his gentleness. She needed a warrior, a man who could fight her demons and win. And if he had to fight her first, that, too, was within his range of power. "No. I'm not going anywhere. Tonight or any other night."

Anger diluted the fear. She had trusted him, she raged silently as her eyes narrowed, her muscles tensing, her strength gathering for another battle. She would not make it easy for him. "I'm not having sex with you."

Killian inhaled deeply, fighting his temper for the insult she had thrown at him. When he knew he could speak without cursing her, he said, "I'm not asking you to." He glared down at her. "In fact, I've never felt less like having sex in my life. It's answers I want and you know it. So don't pretend it's your gorgeous body that got me here. You were moaning, loud enough for me to hear you next door. I want to know why and you're going to tell me."

"Like hell I am." She arched up, infuriated now, the fear fading with his demand.

Killian ignored the wasted effort. "Tell me about the nightmares. Share them with me. Let me help you fight them."

"I don't need your help," she panted, hating the ease with which he controlled her. No man held her against her will. Yet, even as she fought him, she realized his hands caused no pain, his body took no liberties beyond chaining her in place. His eyes held no lust, no demand for an intimacy that she couldn't bear.

"Liar."

The word was a sword that threatened what the hand did not. Silke froze, damming the sudden need in her to surrender, to let Killian share her memories. The moment the idea was recognized, she bucked hard beneath him, panicked now at her own weakness rather than a man's strength.

Killian held her still. "You're not going to win. I can hold you like this all night. I'm not going."

"Then stay, damn you. I still won't tell you anything." If she couldn't send him away physically, she could escape him mentally.

"Tell me about your real mother." If Killian had tightened the last screw on a torture rack, he couldn't have gotten a more pronounced effect for his shot in the dark.

Silke paled, her breath suspended with the pain that he had unleashed. "Stop psychoanalyzing me," Silke breathed roughly.

"What did she do to you?"

Silke clamped her lips shut, glaring at him.

"Were you abused?" He watched her eyes, looking for the truth she would not willingly give. Not one flicker betrayed her. He searched for another angle. He couldn't use the depth of her dossier. He could use only what little the papers had reported over the years, and that hadn't included the references to drugs and alcohol that had been in his report on her early home life. As he thought, he lightly stroked the taut muscles of her throat, gentling her.

Silke held herself silent, waiting, poised to deflect any effort he made to break through. If she ever got started, she didn't know if she could stop.

"If not her, then a man," he said finally, his gaze intent. "Is that the reason that you respond to no one with any depth of emotion?"

"You're wasting your time."

He shook his head. "No, I'm not. You weren't just afraid when I found you tonight. You were terrified. I want to know why."

"Going to kiss it and make it all better?" she demanded sarcastically.

"No." This time her jibe didn't touch his temper, only his understanding and compassion. "I'm going to hold you while you scream and cry and let the pain out. I'm going to hurt like the fires of hell because you'll be and are hurting just as badly. I'm going to risk having you hate me for forcing you to tell me what terrorizes a survivor like you. And I'm going to wonder, probably for the rest of my life, if I've done the wrong thing in forcing your confidence." Every word was a harsh truth—stark, unforgiving, and inescapable.

Silke stared at him, shocked by vulnerability he had willingly laid at her feet.

His fingers encircled her throat where her pulse raced. "And when it's all over, when we look at the pieces of each of us, I'm going to hold you while we both sleep."

Hell and heaven. He offered her both, asking to share each. No one, not even the family she loved and who loved her, had ever held out such a gift. Tears filled her eyes, overflowing. Anger and temper died in the flood. The fear remained—alive, old and

new. She felt its bite, fought her need to run, and won. She looked
at his face through a blurred mist and reached deep into herself
for the strength to share.

Killian bent his head, sipping at the bittersweet moisture.

His caress unlocked her words. "Let me hold you. Then maybe
I can tell you," she whispered shakily. She watched him closely,
knowing that rejection right this moment would kill something in
her that she might never know again.

Killian raised his head, holding her eyes as he slowly released
her hands. When she just wrapped her arms around him, holding
on to him as though she really needed his touch, he sighed deeply.
One battle over. "Take your time. We have all night," he said
softly, settling her more closely to him and himself more comfortably on the pillows. He tucked her head against his bare chest,
waiting.

Silke inhaled his scent, feeling safe as she had never felt. For
a moment she almost drew back from what she was about to do.
There was a very real risk that Killian would not be able to take
what she had to say. Then she thought of his promise. His honesty.
His strength. She had to believe. He had taught her she could.

"I never knew my father. I don't think my mother did either,
at least not for sure. I had two sisters; the younger one was five
years older than I was. We were part of the street scene. My
mother and sisters practiced the oldest profession. They weren't
very good at it, not because they weren't pretty enough but because all three of them had habits that steal youth and clear thinking. They brought the men home at night. I hated it. The noise,
the sounds that made me think someone was being murdered
when I was too young to know what it really meant. Then later,
I hated it because I did know what was going on. My door was
the only one with a lock. I collected coins out of the gutter to
pay for it, and it wasn't much. I had to install it myself, and I
didn't have the right tools and I didn't know what I was doing
anyway. But I felt a little safer. I was always afraid one of the
men would find my room. I didn't sleep at night because I kept
watch. I had this place by the window. I figured if someone got
by the lock I had time to slip out the fire escape and down to
the alley. One night, when I was about eleven, I had to. It was
raining." She glanced toward the windows. "You have no idea

how terrible an alley smells in the rain. I slept in a crate until morning. My sisters thought it was funny. Mother didn't say a word, but from then on I saw her watching me."

Silke shifted uneasily, the image of those faded, hurting eyes still vivid after all these years. She snuggled closer when she felt Killian slide his hands gently up and down her arms, dispelling the chill that the memory brought.

Killian stared straight ahead, washing every vestige of expression from his face. Rage as he had never known filled him. A child. A vulnerable baby at the mercy of that kind of life. If Silke's mother had been there, he wasn't sure he would have been able to keep his hands from around her throat.

"I started to develop about then. I wanted to talk to another woman about what was happening to me, but I was afraid of what my mother or sisters would say or want me to do. So I tried to hide what was happening." She nuzzled his chest, not even realizing she was seeking to burrow deeper into his strength. "But you can't hide that kind of thing. And my mother knew. And she had her own demons, fears. Her habit was growing too strong. She was sick, dying I think. My sisters were too involved with their own habits to care. There was no money, not the kind my mother needed anyway." Silke's hands clenched around Killian's shoulders, her nails digging in. "One night, there was silence. That was more terrible than the sounds. I crept to the door, slipped the lock, and tiptoed out into the tiny hall. Mother's room was the closest. I laid my ear against her door. I had some crazy fear that she had died and no one had told me. But she wasn't dead. She was talking. To the man. He offered her money. At first she didn't want to take it. That surprised me. But he kept talking to her, telling her what he could do for her and for me."

Silke lifted her head, not even aware that tears were raining down her face. "He was buying me for his stable," she said starkly.

Killian swore once, rough and to the point. He pulled her head down, his lips closing over the rest of the words, blotting out the pain if only for an instant of caring. As the child without a haven she had once been, Silke curled against him, taking the comfort he offered. When he lifted his head, he smoothed her hair back with a tender hand. "You have nothing to be ashamed of, Baby. You were a child with no other way to survive."

Silke shook her head, suddenly realizing just what kind of man Killian was. He didn't condemn, judge, or hate her secrets. He accepted them and her just as they were. Her past was her greatest fear, deeper and more consuming than even her memories. He was showing her that it just didn't matter to him what she might have been. For one instant she let herself feel the emotion, bask in the warmth it brought to dispel the cold of the past. Then, as she had learned so long ago, she tucked her treasure out of sight, deep in her mind where no one but she would know what she had found.

"I didn't go. I ran. He didn't get me. No one did. I slept on the streets. I lied to survive. I played the games. I stole to eat, but I didn't sell my body. I never have."

Nine

Killian studied her face, the truth blazing in her golden eyes. Suddenly the facts he had thought he had known about her rearranged themselves yet again. "You were a child," he said, not in disbelief but in shock.

"I was never a child," she replied, her voice so simple, so matter-of-fact that it chilled the room with its statement. "No one could have been in that environment. I learned things about men, women, and their ways of using each other that I took into my thinking before I was mentally old enough to know that even an adult would have had trouble with the knowledge I possessed. There are all kinds of innocence. I have little. Lying to eat, to find shelter, stealing to survive one more day wasn't much different from lying awake at night, protecting myself if need be from the men my mother and sisters brought home. In fact, in some ways, it was a lot easier. At least on the streets I always made sure I could see the enemy coming and I could run."

"How did you get to the St. Jameses?"

"Desperation." Silke looked beyond him for a moment, thinking of those last days on the streets. "The man had people out looking for me. I managed to outrun or outthink most of them for almost a year. But nothing like that could have lasted. There were too many eyes, and he was more furious with every month I escaped him. No one ever had before. I had a friend, an older woman who had been on the streets for about fifteen years. She knew things about everyone, the best places to hide, the safer places to panhandle. She taught me, shared what she had, and when I got quick and slick enough to get more than she did, I returned the favor. But I made a mistake. I forgot that survival doesn't allow for things like honesty and trust. She sold me out to the man."

"Damn her to hell."

Silke focused on his face, the rage burning for her in his eyes. "No. She was sick, in a lot of pain. The man had drugs to take the pain away and give her peace in a world where there was no peace, no release from the hell of hurting until you can't control the scream."

"You can forgive her?" he demanded, knowing in his mind there was no forgiveness for the crime that the other woman had committed.

"I might have done the same in her place."

Killian shook his head, rejecting the idea before she had drawn a breath after the last word. He had learned enough in the days of knowing Silke to realize that would never have been her truth. "No way."

Silke touched his face, stunned at his refusal to see her in a lesser light. No one had ever believed in her honor before. No one. "You can't know that."

He cupped her cheek, looking into her tawny eyes, liking the feel of her in his hands. "Wrong. I know you."

She searched his face, seeing the sincerity but still having trouble believing in it. "Aren't you forgetting my reputation?"

His gaze didn't waver. "We'll get to that one of these days. You will tell me exactly what you've been up to and why you've destroyed your own name. But right now, we're dealing with this bogeyman. Finish your story."

Shaken by the surety in his voice, Silke had to swallow back the words of gratitude that lay on her tongue. Emotion that she had always dammed up filled the silence of her mind. The distance she had always kept between her and the rest of the world had never been so difficult to maintain. "There isn't much more."

"Finish, Silke," he repeated quietly.

She looked away from him for a moment, gathering herself for the last. The worst was over, really. "I found out about the trap. Actually, one of the kids I knew approached me with the information and I paid for it. I ran. There was nowhere left for me to hide in the world I had always known, so I hightailed it across town. I had some mad idea of setting up again. Only I didn't realize that the police were a lot more active in the area I had chosen. I couldn't stay in one place long enough to do anything. I couldn't panhandle either. And stealing was impossible unless I wanted to go in for the kind of thievery that would have done more than get me a slap on the wrist. On top of that, what little money I had was gone and I was hungry and winter was coming." She shivered.

Killian reached down and dragged the comforter up around her shoulders. It was poor comfort against the cold of her memories, but it was all he had.

She smiled faintly at the gesture even as she snuggled into the warmth. "Going to be my keeper, Killian?" she asked softly.

No, going to be your lover, Killian wanted to say but didn't. His body knew its mate. But there was a long road to travel before they would share the pleasure he knew waited at the end of the journey.

"You, more than any other person I have ever encountered, least need a keeper. You'd resent me like hell if I tried," he said instead. "But I wouldn't mind being your friend, a friend you could really trust not to sell you out." Friendship was such a small part of what he wanted from her, but at this moment it was all he thought she could handle.

"I think you are my friend," Silke murmured, examining the idea and finding that she liked it very much. A more intimate demand would have hurt right now. But friendship seemed important, something she had never experienced in the way he was offering it. "But I don't know if I can believe in that kind of trust." There was sadness and cynicism in the curve of her lips.

Her eyes silently asked his forgiveness for her rejection of the last half of his gift.

Killian smoothed the lines from her brow. "Don't worry about it, Silke. It's enough for now. The rest will come. I don't mind proving to you that you can trust me." Even as he said the words, the reality of what he had allowed himself to forget for a time intruded. Although he hadn't lied to Silke, she didn't know the role he had been assigned in her life. But he had time. And time gave moments of closeness when all things were possible. He would have to wait, watch for his moment, and then he could finish the old and begin the new.

"You shouldn't have to prove . . ."

Silke got no farther. Killian covered her mouth with his fingers. "This is our game and we make the rules. You need proof. If I were you, I would, too. That's fair, to us both. And we have time. All the time we want for whatever we need."

"All of this for friendship?" Her brows rose, curious despite the wariness that was so ingrained.

"My kind of friendship, definitely." He stroked the elegant curve of one brow, smiling at her. "Come on and finish your story so we can get to the holding part."

Caught off guard by his teasing, Silke laughed, her body finally softening to his without reservation. "You are holding me," she pointed out, glancing down at their entwined limbs.

"But not like I intend to so that we both can sleep."

"Oh!"

It was his turn to laugh. "Yes, oh." He settled her back into position, her head on his shoulder, his arms wrapped around her. He didn't really care how she lay against him. What he did care about was keeping his emotions as tightly under wraps as necessary, so as not to hurt her any more than she had already been hurt. He couldn't stop the pain that went with her memories, but he would have damned himself in a hell of his own making before he added one single second of hurt to what she had already survived.

"You were out of money," he prompted.

"Feeling like I would never get warm again. I was wandering the streets looking for a place for the night. I saw this huge house with all kinds of lights blazing. There were trees around it, a yard with swings and things. It was the most beautiful thing I had ever seen, and suddenly I hated the family who lived in it as I had never hated anyone in my life. They had everything and I had nothing. I must have stood there for ten minutes before I saw the sign. It wasn't a private home at all. It was one of those shelter things."

Killian kept his hold light, although he wanted to absorb her into his strength. The first part of her story had held so little emotion in spite of the horror of it. Yet this last was filled with the pain, the bitterness, and the fury of denial of the good in life that the child she had been must have suffered that cold night.

"I can remember holding on to the bars of the grilled fence around the yard until my hands hurt. I heard a car come around the corner. I looked over my shoulder. It was the police. Before I could run, a hand wrapped around my wrist, and this girl, the same age as I was, yanked me through the fence. I didn't even realize that I had been holding on to the gate, not the fence itself. That's how I met Caprice, my sister. And through her, I met Lorraine and ended up adopted as a St. James." Silke sighed deeply as she finished. She was warm, suddenly tired as though she had used the last ounce of her energy. Her lashes drifted shut as she inhaled softly, taking in Killian's scent as her next breath. "Caprice has always said that she picked me out to join the family," she murmured.

Killian heard the exhaustion in Silke's voice, the faint slurring of her words as she fought her body's need to rest. He stroked the bright fall of hair, his fingers sliding into the silken flames to massage her scalp, the back of her neck, and down her shoulders. Her purring moan of pleasure was more than a reward. He leaned his cheek against her hair, feeling her grow heavier against him as she relaxed.

Silke frowned slightly as she felt the inky darkness of slumber drift over her. There was something she had to say to Killian. She forced her mind to function, dragging from it the memory of the beginning of her story. "Now, we can be real friends," she murmured, struggling without succeeding in opening her eyes.

Killian's hand hesitated for a split instant in its gentle sweeps. Rage rippled across his face, self-directed, hot and damning. His challenge had been the reason she had relived that horror. His words had opened the floodgates to her past and its agony. He hadn't lied when he had said he would pay for what he was asking of her. Hell was cold compared to his condemnation of himself.

"Very real friends," he whispered rawly, tears such as he had never felt adding a sheen to his blue eyes. "The kind of friends who are safe with each other."

Silke smiled faintly, pleased that she had begun to be the friend he wanted. Maybe complete trust wasn't so very far away after all, she thought as she slipped into sleep.

"Are you certain about this, Raymond?" Geoffrey demanded, his face tight with tension and anxiety. "Your men are positive that their informers have it right?"

Raymond, the chief of police, sighed deeply, wishing that anyone but him had to tell this man that one of his children was in very great danger. "We're as certain as we can be in a situation like this. You'd better alert Carpenter. Thank God you and Lorraine had the good sense to make sure the girls were protected. At least Carpenter is one of the best men I know for this kind of thing."

"What about police protection?"

"We're working on that right now. The thing is, the more people who know, the more chances for a leak. Right now, all our man can be sure of is that Silke is in Atlanta. He doesn't know where, and I damn well want to keep it that way."

Silke rolled over in her sleep, muttering fretfully at the sudden imprisonment of her movements. "Let go," she mumbled, plucking at the arm that held her captive to the bed. The weight triggered her fears as she was pulled even closer to a source of heat. "No!" She struggled in the darkness, her eyes still closed, caught in the dream-reality limbo that allowed all things to be possible. Her nails dug into flesh. Her mouth opened to scream for the help she knew wouldn't come.

Killian awoke slowly, a first for him. The darkness was complete, but the silence was not. Silke was fighting him, her breath labored as she tried to escape their bed. He released her enough to let her know that she was no longer trapped against him, but he didn't let her go completely.

"Easy, Silke," Killian murmured, turning toward her, one hand brushing back the hair from her face. Her skin was hot. He frowned even as he continued to whisper soothing phrases that had little real verbal meaning.

Silke fought the touch for a second before Killian's voice penetrated the nightmare. Her lashes flickered, then opened to the lightless world. "Killian?" His name emerged on a breath of panic she didn't hear as she reached for him instead of fighting to be free of his hold.

"In the flesh," Killian said deeply, sliding his arms under her and lifting her up onto his chest as he rolled onto his back. He stroked her spine, the tense muscles that spoke of her fear, her nightmare hell that demanded more than she could give. "It's almost four. You've slept a long time for your first night."

Silke listened to his words, hearing the reassurance, the pride in her small accomplishment. Her fingers tightened on his shoulders but she didn't notice. "But I woke up screaming."

"My name."

Two words. Simple. Too telling to be denied even had she wanted to do so. "Yes," she agreed, the fear sliding away to be replaced with the security of his touch. "And you were there."

Killian's body flexed, the need he hadn't noticed until this second growing stronger, more demanding. Possession. So easy with some women. So impossible with this one. She couldn't be taken. She had to be given, by herself, by the passion that was maturing even now in the silence. Threading his fingers in her hair, he exerted enough pressure to bring her lips closer. "Are you very sleepy?" he asked softly.

As Silke's eyes adjusted to the darkness, she could see a little of Killian's expression. But it was his voice that told the story of desire chained to his demand. "No," she answered slowly as she brought her hands to his face to frame the strong bones as she bent her head even lower. "Make love to me."

He nipped lightly at her lips, teasing the bottom one for an instant before moving on to the top. "Not all the way tonight. But just a little pleasure to pass the time until dawn."

Not expecting the answer, Silke lifted her head, feeling his fingers slide through her hair as though they were handling satin streamers. "Why?"

"I told you. I want you strong, not frightened, not grateful, not weakened by the past. When we come together, we will come as we are. Equal but different. Less and it devalues what we will have."

"You're so sure."

He stroked her lips with his forefinger, outlining them delicately. "So are you or you would never have shared your past with me."

Silke kissed the tip of his finger, then leaned down for the kiss she was determined to have. "Pleasure until dawn." She bit lightly at his chin, her teeth marking but not breaking the skin. "That's two hours away, give or take."

He chuckled softly, hearing the challenge. "And you'll break me if you can."

Her golden eyes gleamed in the darkness. "I'll do my poor best," she agreed huskily.

Killian settled her more intimately between his thighs, then wrapped his legs around the back of hers so that she couldn't escape.

She laughed softly in the darkness, no longer interested in getting away. "Good move, Killian," she breathed as she rotated her hips in a way that caught him unprepared. His groan of need deepened her amusement and her desire. Her hands slid down his body, teaching him the points that held the most need of her dancing, teasing touch.

"Damn you, Silke. Play fair."

She shook back her hair, the game feeding something wild in her. She wanted him to shatter in her arms, to shout her name to the heavens as she granted him the release that only her body, her loving could provide. A shocking admission in the silence of her mind, but she didn't turn from its truth. She wanted to mark Killian as her own, to hold him near for as long as the fire between them burned.

"I am not playing," she whispered roughly as she nipped at his ear, tracing the whorls, blowing gently as she explored the spot behind his lobe.

Power flowed into her with each new caress. She was seductress, drunk with her knowledge, her gift of pleasure for the mate she had chosen. As she eased over him, her gown rode high over her hips. She moved, deepening the contact between them as her flesh warmed him in spite of the briefs that shielded him from the final mating that she was beginning to need more than her next breath.

Killian felt the change in her, stunned at the game that had suddenly developed into something far more risky, far more enthralling than he had thought could exist between a man and a woman. She was fire, greedy, hot, and out of control. Her body flowed over his, molding to his shape, redesigning his desire for her. Passion soared, slipping past the restraint and control that had always been his. His hands tightened on her sinuous length, guiding instead of chaining. Fire burning cupped in his hands, heaven waiting breathing kisses over his chest. Peace never. Challenge issued and accepted. His fingers waltzed lower, digging gently into the base of her spine and the nerves hidden there. He pressed deep, drawing small circles that beguiled and enslaved.

Silke reared back, her eyes pagan as she moaned her pleasure. Her hips pressed down into his, once, twice, three times. Thrust. Parry. Demand. Give.

"More?" he asked, pulling her head down with one hand as his caresses moved lower, sliding around her hips to the place where they lay as close as a heartbeat.

"Yes," she groaned when he found the center of her need, touching her so delicately that the pleasure burst forth in a flood of sensation. She bucked, her neck arched, her back straight, her hands flattened on his chest for more leverage.

Killian breathed in her scent as his lips found her breasts through the fabric of her gown. Her nipples were hard points in a body so soft that he could lose himself in the silken bonds.

Silke held him to her, letting him touch her as she had allowed no man. "Pleasure," she whimpered, arching ever closer.

"Heaven," he replied, pulling the gown over her head in one smooth motion.

"Not fair." She pulled at his briefs, losing the battle with the fabric when he didn't help her.

"You want me. You'll have to make it happen." This time the challenge was his.

Silke's eyes glittered with intent as she suddenly tipped her body sideways, pulling him over on his side before he could brace himself. She slipped her hands under the rim of his briefs, slid them down, releasing the shaft that was readying itself for her. "My point," she whispered boldly, stroking his length, feeling him shudder against her as she had done when he had taken her breasts into his mouth.

"Score keeping?" He rolled onto his back, lifting her high enough so that she couldn't quite reach him. While he protected that region, Silke claimed another.

His nipples were as sensitive as her own and just as vulnerable. Each peak hardened for her, begging for her kisses.

Suddenly, Killian broke. His hands dug into her flesh for one instant as he accepted the knowledge that this time she was stronger than he, that his desire for this woman was more powerful than any he had ever faced. He arched, ready to mate, to mark her as his. Her name was a curse and a prayer.

Silke looked down, seeing the need out of control, feeling her own desire racing to meet the demand. Whether he pulled her down to be impaled or she met him more than halfway, she didn't know. All she felt was the first tearing pain of total possession.

Killian froze, shocked at what her body had just proclaimed.

Silke cupped his face. "If you stop, I will murder you," she threatened huskily.

"How can you be a virg. . . ."

Her kiss sealed the rest of his question as she deepened their mating, taking his length and demanding more. Killian was a man caught by his own desire and by the woman who fed it. He rose to meet her, giving all she asked, taking what he needed with each stroke. Fire. Heaven and hell. Light for the darkness to die. Her body. Now his. Deeper. More pleasure. More need. Passion. Shimmering on the horizon. His name branding the silence as Silke quivered in his arms a second before he shouted his claim to the night.

Then silence filled with questions.

Killian stroked Silke's back as she lay pillowed on his chest, her body still joined with his. Her scent and the fragrance of their lovemaking wrapped around him, gentling any anger that could have lived in this moment for the deception she had practiced.

"I didn't lie to you," Silke said quietly, rubbing her cheek against his heart, her hands holding him near.

He buried his fingers in her hair, holding her close to his heart when she would have raised her head. "No, but you let me believe a lie." He released her slowly, knowing that the time had come for more answers to the questions that never seemed to end.

She lifted her head, her eyes searching his. "Another story, Killian?"

"Don't you think I deserve to know?" He touched her face, looking for something that he must have missed all this time. The shadows hid a lot, but he didn't need a light to know that there would be nothing in her eyes or her expression to betray her physical innocence. She had learned her lessons too well.

Silke considered her options. She hated lies. Killian did have the right to demand more of her. She had given him that right when she had offered him her untouched body. But equally, there were others to protect.

"I can tell you some of it," she said finally.

Killian frowned at the half-response. Something more than her wariness with others was hidden in her words. "Why?"

"There are others involved. Possibly in danger."

Killian tensed. "Do your parents know?"

She nodded.

Killian had spent too many years living by his instincts. Two and two in this case added to a great deal more than four. Geoffrey had told him a lie. It was that simple. There was no stalker. The knowledge lay in his gut like a stone.

"Start from the beginning," he said finally, quietly.

Silke frowned at the flat tone. The warmth that had lived in his voice was gone. Only cool, clear purpose remained. She shivered at the change, feeling that what had happened between them had just turned into more than pleasure and trust between friends. "What's wrong?"

"Did you think I would accept your being in danger without a blink?" he asked instead of answering her directly.

Silke sighed softly, relieved. Suddenly she didn't feel so cold, so at risk. He cared. Her smile trembled.

For the first time, Killian damned his profession. Her smile was more lethal than a knife in the hand of an expert. But to keep her safe he would brave even that blade.

Ten

Silke curled against his side. It would be easier if she didn't have to look at him when she told him what she had done. "I told you about my mother's drug habit and that of my sisters. But I didn't tell you I grew up to hate what the pills and the needles did to them and to the others that I saw every day. Children who were too young to realize what the danger was. Old people who were too hopeless to try to clean up their lives. My people and the way they lived to support their habit. And my mother, ready to sell her child into a life that was nothing more than a living death. I could have been like them. I could have become one of the maniacal souls who would do or be anything for one more fix. But I escaped. A kind hand of fate for a child who shouldn't have survived. Somehow, that made it worse, not better. I felt guilty for making it out when others could not. I owed a debt. I had to pay it. And one day I got my chance. I overheard something that I shouldn't have. I watched. I waited, and I added together the bits and pieces that came my way. I found a source for the drugs that existed even in the rarefied atmosphere of the world that I had naively thought was clean of the taint of drugs. One anonymous call was all it took to turn in the dealer. But one came after him. I called on him, too. Then another. By then I realized my calls were futile as long as the network existed. So I dug deeper. It wasn't so very hard to slide into the driven crowd of young money. All it took was a swish of my hips, a drooling man on my arm, and a glass of liquor in my hand. No one thought anything of the little orphan Lorraine Dayton-St. James had picked out of the gutter reverting to type.

"Besides I knew all the moves. All I had to do was remember what I had seen my mother and sisters doing. No one paid any attention to what they said in front of me. Most of the time I think they figured I was too sloshed to hear them." She raised her head from his shoulder. "The funny thing is I hate to drink almost as much as I hate drugs. I don't need the high, and I certainly don't want the loss of control."

Killian touched her lips. "I believe you," he murmured quietly.

She smiled faintly. "I needed you to say that," she admitted.

He tucked her head back in its resting place. "I know." He pulled her closer. "Finish it, Silke."

"Anyway, the next time I made one of my phone calls, in spite of the precautions I took, I was found out." She felt him tense against her. "Not by the dealers," she hurried to explain. "But by a man named Hollander. He contacted me through one of his people, a guy named David. Hollander wanted me to work for them to smash the network. By now, I was in too far emotionally to give it up, so I agreed. David was my contact, and because of my reputation, he became my latest escort and later my fiance. In all, three of Hollander's people were engaged to me. He rotated his team as much as he could for all our sakes. A few weeks ago, the last piece of the network fell into our laps. Hollander was almost ready to close in, but the man was getting worried, asking questions that never should have occurred to him. I was at risk and Hollander didn't want to explain away a St. James corpse. Then my mother came up with her scheme to get me away from the dissolute life I was leading. I would have agreed for her sake alone. So, instant escape route. Then I met you." She sighed deeply, glad he knew it all now. Until this moment she hadn't realized what a burden all the secrets she had carried had become.

Killian stared into the darkness, fighting the rage he felt at the unknown Hollander and the risks that Silke had run. He couldn't even mitigate his reaction with the knowledge that Silke had entered into the dark world not realizing what she was getting into. She had known. She had willingly thrown herself into a situation where death could have been a blessing. He had thought he understood her at least a little. Instead, he knew that he had hardly scratched the surface of the woman she was.

"Say something," Silke murmured without raising her head. "Even if you call me a fool for getting involved, say something."

Killian cupped her chin in his hand, lifting her face so that she had to look at him. Dawn was beginning to break across the heavens, filling the room with the soft gray light of a new day. "I don't think you are a fool. I'm not sure what I do think you are."

Silke studied him, seeing the rage banked in his eyes, hearing the sincerity in his voice. She frowned. "Are you angry with me?"

"Maybe, a little." He shifted restlessly. "But more with the situation and the man who let you get in that deep."

She shook her head, relieved that his anger hadn't been turned on her. "He didn't let me do anything. In fact, he hated having me in at all. He was positive I was going to get myself or one of his people killed."

"But you stayed."

"I blackmailed him," she replied starkly. "I threatened to go over his head. My father could have found out who his superior was easily enough. I would have told them what I had stumbled into and how Hollander was going to jeopardize the whole thing to keep me out."

He felt the steel in her, knew she wasn't grandstanding it. She would have carried out her threat. "Your father would have known then. And your mother."

"I would have risked it."

He stared at her, reading the soul-deep purpose in her hammered-gold eyes, the commitment to an ideal that few had the courage to address. "It meant that much to you."

"I always pay my debts. I owed. I paid or died. There was no other choice."

Killian turned her words over in his mind, seeing more than he wanted to know. Silke had honor. Not the modern version that held more gray than white. But the old-fashioned kind that saw the world in hard-edged terms. Right was right regardless of the personal cost. Wrong was unacceptable. And yet this woman had once been a child who had done wrong by society's standards to survive. He didn't want to think what those young, so necessary sins had cost, what scars they had left on her soul.

She touched his face. "Can you understand why I did it?"

He nodded, stunned at the depth he hadn't realized could still exist in her, stunned too at how very much he was coming to need her in his life. "Yes." He copied her gentle, gesture. "Now, tell me why no man has known you."

Silke didn't hesitate. Of all the answers he had asked of her, this was the easiest. "I never met anyone I could trust enough, want enough to give myself to." She leaned closer, her lips tracing his. He had cared enough to let her see what she meant to him. She could do no less. "Until you came, I didn't think I would ever feel safe enough to let myself be this vulnerable."

Her kiss was acid, trust given that he didn't deserve. With the threat that lay over her life, he didn't dare tell her who he was, risking her anger and possible renunciation when she would need his protection the most. Even as the thoughts formed in his mind, even as he felt the yielding of her body, the taste of her mouth, he accepted the cost that laying with her, knowing her, sharing with her would demand of him. Pain lay in his future. The moment when she would look into his eyes as he told her the truth. The second when the trust she gave would turn to a sword to cut out his soul. The reality she had built on the ashes of her past would not allow forgiveness to come easily, if at all. As his arms wrapped around her, he knew that no matter what the future held, what debts he would have to pay, he would have gladly paid tenfold to spare her the disillusionment that would come.

Killian shut the door to the office he had been given at the Douglas Plastics building. He had left Silke downstairs at her desk, settling into her new job. She had been as excited as a child at the prospect, teasing him, when he had driven them to work, with the kind of mistakes she would probably be making all day. He had managed to hold up his end of the conversation despite the fact that he was more concerned about getting in touch with Geoffrey and laying the facts he had before the man he had thought he knew. He dialed the number he had long ago committed to memory.

Geoffrey answered on the second ring. "I thought you would never check in," he said, skipping his usual greeting. It was a measure of his anxiety that his normally controlled voice was alive with worry.

"If I had realized what was really going on, I would have been giving you hourly reports," Killian replied angrily.

Geoffrey sighed deeply, hearing the sting in Killian's words and feeling the wave of temper that went with it despite the physical distance between them. "How did you find out? The police?"

"No. Silke told me."

Geoffrey frowned. He knew his daughter of the heart too well to accept that kind of an announcement without question. "What do you mean she told you? That isn't like her at all. When you first called, you said you had established a personal link with her. Just how personal is it? You were only supposed to guard her, damn it."

Killian bit back a number of useless retaliatory words and settled for milder ones. "That's what I'm trying to do. With both hands and feet tied, I might add. There's a hell of a difference between the kinds of precautions to take with a stalker and a drug lord bent on revenge. She could have been dead by now and you know it."

"What was I supposed to do? Betray her?"

"Yes, if it saved her neck, betray her to hell and back."

Geoffrey raked his fingers through his silvered hair, aware of every one of his years. "I didn't have time to think that far."

"Nice epitaph." Killian wasn't ready to back down. "Death isn't always as simple as a bullet in the head or heart. The man would have made her pay in ways you can't even imagine just for the hell of it and as an example to anyone else. Stick that alongside your scruples and tell me which choice you should have made."

Geoffrey paled. "Damn it, Killian. I made a mistake. I'm not God. She's alive. And she has you."

"And I'm going to keep her that way. Anyone who gets between me and her is dead meat, so make sure that whoever knows understands that. I don't know friends from foes, so it's easiest to get rid of them all. You gave her to me and I'll keep her."

"I want to help. I've got people you can trust to help."

"This isn't your world, Geoffrey. The good guys don't always wear white hats, and money can buy a lot of people, even people who are supposed to be friends. I'm not taking those kind of risks. I'll only trust who I know. No outsiders. I can't afford them. Silke can't afford them." He waited a beat for the reality to settle in, then continued in the same uncompromising tone. "Now, tell me everything you've done and said and to whom since this mess started. I don't care how trivial anything is. I want it."

He reached into the left drawer of the desk and extracted a legal pad to take down the facts as Geoffrey began relating all he had said and done since the day Silke had told him and Lorraine what she had been doing. It took almost an hour of intense interrogation before Killian was satisfied. He hung up on Geoffrey and dialed another number.

A series of clicks indicated the transfer of the first number to another, then another. Finally, a voice answered. It was clipped, dark, and faintly accented.

"Quin, I need you."

"When? Where?"

"Atlanta. As soon as possible."

"How bad?"

"Bad enough. Drugs. A civilian in where she shouldn't be, and it looks as though the woods are full of hunters. I need equipment. Untraceable if anyone is looking, and state of the art."

An immaculate white cuff was shaken back over a scarred arm. A thin Rolex gleamed in the half light of the candlelit room. "By tonight. Ten. Where?"

Killian gave him his address.

"Cover?"

"Friend."

"Easy." Quin lifted the crystal goblet to his lips and let the wine slide delicately down his throat. "Is she pretty?"

Killian almost smiled at the question. Quin had a unique ability to cut through to the heart of the matter. "Heaven and hell."

Quin's light brows rose, silver eyes glittering with emotion he would never have shown if he hadn't been alone. "Then I will like her."

"It won't matter, either way," Killian replied before gently replacing the receiver.

He stared into space, thinking about the man he had just called. Silke paid her debts and so did he. His world was as filled with gray as her own. Quin was one of those gray shadows. Once an enemy, then through a stroke of fate and a bullet, a friend. They had a strange alliance. A phone call brought help but never simply an exchange between friends. Quin had no friends that Killian knew. He was beyond being a loner. He was truly an island. He came and went on a whim. He diced with death if he was in the mood, and he owed his allegiance to no country. Killian knew little beyond the facts in a file he had once been given, facts he was certain were lies cleverly disguised as truths. Whatever lay in Quin's past would always belong to him alone. But whatever Quin wasn't, there was one thing he was. He was a guarantee that Silke would live. Had he been hired by the man trying to kill Silke, he would have been the promise that she would die.

Silke frowned at the switchboard in front of her, trying to keep the directions for its use straight in her mind. She was determined to do this job right. The smiling part was natural, the stock greetings were easy, but this high-tech creation made the whole thing seem like an elaborate plot to show her ineptitude.

"You're going to give yourself wrinkles."

Silke glanced up, grinning at Killian as he leaned his elbows on her desk. "Have you ever worked one of these?"

He looked at the light-dotted board and shook his head. "No. Why?"

"Mike's secretary just spent the last hour sitting with me while I supposedly got the hang of it. So far this morning, I've cut off two people, connected three to the wrong place, and put someone on hold for four minutes."

"The last doesn't sound too bad."

She laughed huskily. "Trust me, that was the worst of the lot. The guy on hold was the boss."

Killian shook his head, laughing in spite of the worry dogging his footsteps. With the sun pouring in through the skylights overhead, the sound of Silke's amusement dancing in the air, and the vivid life brightening her eyes, it was difficult to remember how close they were waltzing to death. "Did he blister your ears?"

"No. He was rather nice actually, although I couldn't tell if he was gritting his teeth while he was explaining that he really didn't want his associates and customers to hang on for longer than a moment."

Killian started to reach out to her, but the board pinged lightly, drawing Silke's attention. Killian watched her deal with the caller. She was working carefully, her eyes clear with a need to succeed. He wanted to cuddle her close, telling her that she didn't need to worry, that she would get the hang of the job in no time. Passion had driven him so hotly only hours before. Yet now, looking at her, he felt something deeper, gentler, fuller. He straightened, startled at the richness of the emotion. Desire he understood. Friendship. Trust. Passion. But not this.

Silke made the appropriate connection and glanced back to Killian only to find him walking away. "Killian?" she called softly.

He looked over his shoulder, avoiding the question in her eyes. "I'll be down to pick you up for lunch at twelve thirty."

"Ready for lunch?" Mike's secretary tapped Silke on the shoulder, smiling as Silke fielded another call, routing it without mishap. "You're sure doing better than I did with that thing," she added frankly when Silke rotated in her chair to look at her.

"You had trouble, too?"

The older woman nodded. "Did I ever. I told Mike if he didn't get someone in here to take over I was quitting. That thing gave me more nightmares than any boss I've ever had."

Laughing, Silke rose and handed over the headset that went with the job. "Thanks for telling me that. I had the feeling that I was the only person in the universe being intimidated by a switchboard."

The secretary took Silke's place. "First jobs are always tough, but you're doing fine." She inclined her head toward the main elevators. "Here comes your escort. I wish I believed in poaching," she murmured. "No wonder the female contingency in this building is suddenly finding ways to stop in and welcome us all to Atlanta. And here I thought it was the famous Southern hospitality."

Silke grinned, her eyes dancing as she exchanged a woman-to-woman look with secretary. "I'll tell him you said that."

"Don't you dare."

Killian's brows rose as he got close enough to hear the last. "Tell me what?" He looked from Silke's wicked smile to the woman beside her.

The secretary groaned, taking refuge in handling a call. Silke slipped from behind the main desk, pausing only to collect her handbag. "It's girl talk. Nothing that you should worry about."

"Your tone is enough to make that comment a lie of the first order," he replied as they stepped onto the sidewalk and the heat of midday surrounded them. He tucked her arm in his even as he scanned the area for anyone showing undue interest in their activities. Although there had been no indication of direct danger to Silke as yet from any of the contacts he had spent the morning investigating, he was going to operate on the premise that there was.

They walked the short distance to the parking garage in silence. Silke's amusement died slowly as she realized that Killian seemed worried. "What's wrong?" she asked the moment he joined her in the car. "Are there problems already? Something with security?"

Startled, Killian's hand stilled before he could start the car. "Why do you say that?"

"Mainly because you looked like you were inspecting every building for snipers when we were out in the open." She shrugged, suddenly uneasy at the way he was studying her. The years she had spent watching every shadow, protecting her own back and those with whom she worked had heightened her senses, maybe even oversensitized them.

"It's my job to make certain that this place is secure," he said finally.

Silke examined the answer, realizing in a second that it told her nothing. Her uneasiness deepened, instincts that had kept her alive rose to the occasion. "No, it's more than that," she said slowly, scanning his face for any betraying flicker.

Killian made himself turn away from those suddenly shrewd eyes. The quick way she had picked up on his preoccupation was something he hadn't foreseen and he should have. The danger in which she had stood for the last few years would have given her an alertness that another woman wouldn't have possessed. Mentally cursing his lapse, he set about retrieving the situation.

"You're right. It is more than that. Our boss is worried about this move. There has been trouble at the main plant. Accidents that shouldn't have happened. Small things, but the kinds of situations that make workers very worried. He doesn't want a repeat here." As far as it went, Killian told the truth.

Silke frowned at the information. The sincerity in his voice obvious, but she couldn't shake the feeling he wasn't telling her the whole truth. The thought disturbed her. She had trusted Killian enough to tell him her life story. She had trusted him enough to give herself to him in passion. So why was she suddenly assailed with doubts? Were they real, or products of the years that had gone before?

Eleven

Killian touched her face, stroking away the tiny lines of worry that had formed on her brow. If there had been another way to divert her, if the fragile trust they had established had had more time to develop, he wouldn't do what he was about to do. "Smile for me, Silke," he murmured, leaning across to tease her lips. He nipped gently at the bottom one, feeling the shiver of response that ran through her. Even as his own body reacted, his mind called him a betrayer. "This is our hour. Let's not think about work."

Silke felt his heat, the passion that simmered in his words. Her body remembered the pleasure he had taught it so well to hold out for long. Her hands rose, cradling his head as his fingers slipped down her throat, circling her neck where her pulse beat in time to each of his kisses. "Killian?" she murmured huskily, letting the sweetness of his subtle seduction flow over her. Her doubts faded as her limbs molded to his.

"Yes, Silke," he breathed, inhaling her scent, remembering the way she had yielded to him in the hours before dawn. For as long as it lasted, for as long as the lie held them bound in this fantasy world, he would give her every ounce of joy of which he was capable. It would not lessen the pain when it came, not for either of them, but maybe, if all his prayers were answered, these memories would be the bridge over the chasm of lies he lived to keep her safe.

He touched her breasts lightly through the silk of her blouse and the lace of her bra. She shuddered in his arms, her mouth opening beneath his. The semilight of the covered garage was a private haven that was alive with possibilities. He could take her here, lift her across the seat and onto his lap. His need was great. Hers, too. A joining and sweet heaven to be found in silken bonds of her body. But in this it was her choice. He couldn't protect her against the lie he lived, but he could offer her the control of what would happen between them.

"Here?" He traced the hard nipple embraced in lace and silk. "Do you want me here?"

The rough, tortured sound of his voice brought Silke's head up, her eyes half closed with the force of the passion rising within her. "We can't."

"We could. It's private, dark, and ours." He lowered his mouth, tracing her lips, teasing them open again. "Or I can take you home."

Temptation was man. This man. Silke drank of his taste, his feel, his need as she arched closer. With her last ounce of sanity she made her decision. "Home," she whispered deeply even as her fingers slipped between the buttons of his shirt to his chest. He jerked in her arms, caught by her caress. She smiled wickedly.

Killian's hands tightened as he fought to give her what she asked. He raised his head, inhaled deeply, his senses filling with her scent. "If you value our lives, sit over there and don't make a move." He caught her shoulders, pushing her back to her side of the car. "And whatever you do, don't forget where we are."

Silke could feel the tremors of need unfulfilled racing through her, but she didn't care. Killian had taken them to the edge of madness, but for her sake had pulled them back. Within her, one more barrier fell victim to his honor, another level of trust was born.

Killian looked at her for a moment before he started the car. His hands were shaking but he didn't care. It was the expression on her face that held him. The walls she had built were falling. The knowledge was both acid and ambrosia.

"Hurry," Silke prompted.

Killian made himself smile as he turned from her. If trials of fire were to temper the soul, his would be pure beyond all recognition before his time with Silke was done.

"I will," he replied starkly.

The drive was short and silent. Neither wanted to break the mood. Both held the memory of the night as a talisman for different reasons. They didn't touch as they mounted the stairs to the second floor of the apartment quad. As before, they chose her bed rather than his.

Killian closed the door of the bedroom and took her in his

arms. Silke started to unbutton her blouse, conscious of how little time they had. Killian stopped her.

"My privilege."

She smiled, feeling treasured as he released the first button. "Only if I get to return the favor."

"Gladly," he whispered as the first inch of her ivory skin was freed for his gaze. Another button fell victim. Then another. He felt the cool air touch his own skin at the same moment he pushed the blouse from her shoulders. He traced the edge of her bra, teasing them both while the hunger in him raged. His eyes glittered behind his black lashes. "If I had drawn a picture of the ideal woman, I would have missed you completely."

Silke stroked his shoulders, reclaiming the sweeps of muscles that were so hard and yet showed her such tenderness. "I know I'm not ideal."

He cupped her lace-covered breasts and brought them home to the thick hair that shielded his chest. "That's not what I meant. My imagination wouldn't have done you justice."

Silke stilled, shocked by the depth of emotion in his dark voice. "You mean that," she whispered, awed and humbled at the same time. "You can't mean that."

"But I do. Your past hasn't marked you with ugliness as you seem to think. It has given you a clarity that is rare, precious. I hate the pain that it caused you, but I respect and admire the woman born in that hell. She is very beautiful, all the way to her soul."

Tears that were so hard for Silke to shed formed in her eyes, overflowing in crystaline streams of release that she hadn't realized she needed. Just that silently, just that easily, another wall came down.

"Thank you."

He dipped his fingertips into the moisture beading on her skin and took it to his mouth. "No, thank you for sharing yourself with me." He looked into her eyes, for one second succumbing to the need to take something for himself, to hold one small hostage to the future. "And if, one day, I hurt you, remember that this was my truth of you."

Silke frowned at the certainty underlying his words, the pain that lay in his eyes, pain that was stronger for an instant than the desire that bound them. She touched his face. "I can't believe you will hurt me, not knowingly," she said huskily, the trust he had taught her driving the rebuttal. His smile was the saddest thing she had ever seen. Fear laced through her, fear for him and herself. "Can't you tell me?"

He shook his head. "I wish I could," he admitted finally, honestly.

Silke searched his face for the strength that was never far from the surface. Her instincts were working again, warning of a danger that she couldn't see, and yet, as she studied him, seeing the way he made no attempt to evade her gaze, she couldn't make herself believe that he was any kind of a threat to her.

"We're using up our hour," she said softly, at last.

He sighed deeply, relieved yet frustrated in a way that had nothing to do with his libido. "So we are," he agreed, swinging her into his arms before she realized what he intended. He carried her to the bed, dropping on one knee in the center to deposit her gently in the covers.

Silke looked up at him, glad she hadn't asked for more information. It was becoming a point of honor for her to trust him. "We aren't going to have much fun with this many clothes," she whispered throatily.

His smile was an invitation and a challenge. "Then take off what you want and I'll do the same." He slid his hands beneath her to unhook her bra, freeing her breasts in an ivory spill for his appreciation.

Silke was busy with her own appreciation. She slid the suit jacket and shirt off his shoulders as one garment, baring him completely from the waist up. Her fingers tangled in the thicket of dark hair that could tantalize and warm her skin at the same time. She hadn't known the male form could hold so much beauty, so much sensual pleasure. His scent was seductive, demanding that she inhale deeply and often. Her lips were dry with anticipation, need. Her tongue peeked out, moistening them.

Killian groaned at the unconsciously provocative action. Everything about Silke was made to inflame his need, from the way her fingers curled like tiny, gentle claws in his flesh, the way her body seemed to fit so perfectly to his, to the way her mouth promised delight with something as simple as a kiss. "An hour isn't going to be long enough," he groaned, taking her mouth, kissing her deeply, letting her feel the full spectrum of his desire.

Silke responded, her arms around his neck, her legs tangled with his. Their clothes vanished somehow. The sheets rippled and slid off the bed as they twisted together in the ancient mating dance that was brand-new because it was made just for them. He pleasured her, whispered dark words of need and joy in her ears. She breathed his name, her own litany of delight to mark every claim he made on her body. And when they were one, the sun shone in the room, its heat far cooler than the desire that drove them to cry out at the final moment of true marriage. And when it was over, Silke lay curled on his chest, her ear pressed against his thundering heart, his arms around her, locking out the world. She was high on the feel of him. She was as light as a cloud and as free as the wind. He had given her wings and taught her how to use them.

"I wish we didn't have to go back to work," Killian murmured into her bright hair.

She rubbed her forehead against his chin. "So do I." She kissed the hollow in his throat, laughing softly when he shuddered. "Why is it that the more we have the more I want?"

He smiled faintly. "I don't know. But if you find out, tell me."

She raised her head to look at him. "Has it been like this for you before?" The moment the question was out, Silke regretted it.

Killian lightly touched the lines of her frown, smoothing them away. "You have the right to ask," he said quietly, accurately guessing the cause. "I gave it to you when I asked for a share in your past." He cupped her chin and kissed her deeply. The one secret he held would be the only one between them. "Ask me anything and I will tell you," he promised when he freed her mouth.

Her lips curved slightly, then her smile grew in strength and joy. Her eyes lit with more than passion. A desire to tease added a wicked sparkle. "You mean you will kiss and tell for me?"

He grinned. "Well, not quite that. I try to be a gentleman whenever possible." He sat up in bed, bringing her with him. "And besides, you and I have to be back to work or we'll both be out of a job. You make a list of your questions and you can grill me tonight over dinner." He kissed her one final time and then set her on her feet.

Silke trailed her fingers down his chest, leaving her invisible brand in the wake of her teasing fingertips. "Will you think of me this afternoon?"

He rose, his body gilded by the sun pouring in the windows. "I'm going to try my best not to, just so I can get some work done." He patted her bottom and pointed her in the direction of her scattered clothes.

Silke added an extra sway in her hips as she took the two steps necessary to bring them within reach. She grinned to herself at Killian's bitten-off oath.

"Woman, you should be outlawed."

Silke glanced over her shoulder. "Then you could be the bounty hunter sent to bring me in. Do you think I would bring a hefty reward?"

Killian felt the teasing comment all the way to the soles of his feet. He leaned down and picked up his pants. "I think you'd bring the biggest on record," he said, as he straightened. He looked not at her, but at his slacks as he pulled them on.

Silke laughed, pleased with his reply. She wanted to be valuable in his eyes, more precious than anything he had ever held. "For that I will cook you a really special meal with my first paycheck."

Killian had never felt less like laughing, but he did it anyway. He had made his choices. He wouldn't balk because he found them costing him more with every passing second.

"Have you found her yet?"

"I'm working on it, boss. We've discovered where she's working but not where she's living. I've got a man stationed at Douglas Plastics to follow her home tonight. She's riding with this guy who heads up the security team. A new guy. Do you want me to check him out, too?"

"Don't be a fool. Anyone around Silke St. James is important. But more importantly, time is running out. The net is tightening. Get rid of this woman before the week is out and make it good. I want the kind of example that will make the whole town clam up."

Spano pressed his fingers together as he held the gaze of the man he had summoned to help him eliminate one of the sources that had brought his carefully constructed empire to the brink of ruin. No one threatened him, no one.

"If she lives past Sunday, there won't be a place you can hide where I won't find you."

The hireling swallowed hard, trying not to let the effect of the softly spoken words show on his face. "I won't let you down," he promised.

Spano nodded, then waved one slender hand toward the door. He waited a beat while his associate rose to leave. When his back was to him, Spano spoke one more time. "Take the man with her out if there is the least question of his affiliation. Don't worry about the tab. Do the job right and I'll remember."

"Thanks, boss."

Killian leaned back in his chair, his face set in harsh lines of contemplation. The hours until Quin's arrival were trickling away, and the information he had been able to gather so far was a long way from being reassuring. He had contacts in a number of fields, many of them not quite legal. Although he hadn't been able to confirm it as yet, there was at least one tracker in town and possibly a contract man as well. Silke's sands of life were racing through the hourglass. And his hands were tied. He didn't dare leave her unprotected to fade into the shadowy world where death was cheap and information expensive. That was where Quin would come in. He could move in those nether regions and, because he was unofficial, could also, with the application of his own brand of tricks, become untraceable. Quin was Silke's edge as well as his. Killian glanced at his watch, grimacing at the slow drip of time. Only a few more hours, he reminded himself.

"That's the fourth time you've looked at your watch," Silke murmured between sips of the excellent vintage of wine Killian had insisted was necessary to do justice to the meal she had cooked.

Killian glanced up, shrugging. "That's because I have a friend coming by tonight and he's running late," he replied.

Silke's brows rose. "Why didn't you say anything before?"

"Why?"

He laughed, amusement lightening his worry for a moment. "Mainly because Randall Quinlan has to be experienced to be appreciated."

"That's sounds vaguely ominous."

"Oh, Quin's that all right. And a thousand other things as well."

Silke settled deeper into the pillows at the head of Killian's bed. Until they had time to go shopping, his bed or hers doubled as every piece of furniture they had yet to acquire, including a dining table. "What kinds of things?" she asked curiously, intrigued by the tone in Killian's voice.

He shook his head before setting his wineglass aside and stretching out alongside her. He plucked her flute out of her hand and set it next to his. "I won't tell you. I don't want to spoil the effect." He nuzzled her throat, tracing patterns on her skin with the tip of his tongue.

Silke quivered with each caress. "We're spending a lot of time in bed," she murmured, lifting her chin to allow him more access to her neck.

"Are you saying you're not enjoying yourself?"

She laughed at the idea. "No, but I hope your friend isn't going to keep leaning on the doorbell."

Killian raised his head and swore. He had been so wrapped up in her that he hadn't really registered the buzzing that now seemed to fill the apartment. "One of the things I left out is that Quin has very little patience with things technical." He pushed off the bed, raked his fingers through his hair, and cast one look over her. "Try to look as though we haven't been doing what we have just been doing," he muttered before stalking out of the room.

Silke grinned as she straightened her dress, tugging the off-the-shoulder-style bodice up to a more discreet line. She had just time enough to tuck her legs under her Indian style before Killian returned with the tallest man she had ever seen off a basketball court. He was easily six seven or eight. His hair was a mixture of so many light colors that one couldn't have called it either blond or silver. His eyes were pewter, cool, analytical. He moved like water flowing over rough ground, silent, totally fluid. If the word "danger" had a physical manifestation, this was the man. Yet Silke felt no fear. Whatever else this man might be, he was no threat to her. Her smile broke, the curve of her lips the gesture that had brought more than one man to his knees.

Quin glanced sideways at his friend. "You were right. Definitely, heaven and hell."

Killian shook his head, amused at the silent assessment that had gone on between Silke and Quin.

"Is that the way he described me to you?" Silke asked after a second.

Quin looked at her, his lips twitching at the corners for a smile that never answered her own. "The only way he described you," he agreed in his darkest voice.

Silke considered that, finding she liked it very much. She looked at Killian, intrigued to discover that, although Quin physically dwarfed her lover, he certainly didn't diminish the aura of power that seemed to surround Killian. If she had had to choose an ally in a battle, she would have wanted Killian at her back first and Quin second.

Twelve

Quin glanced around the empty room. "You have an interesting decorator. He or she hits the important stuff first. But at least there could have been a chair or two."

Killian gestured toward the end of the bed. "It's either that or the floor. I haven't had a chance to shop for furniture yet. Neither has Silke."

Silke grinned. "I promise you there aren't any crumbs in the bed, although we are eating our meals here at the moment."

Quin arranged himself on one corner of the foot, inwardly amused that Killian managed to get between him and Silke and still not impair their line of vision. "I was thinking about trying to steal a bed for a day or two, but you don't have an extra," he murmured, looking Killian in the eye.

Killian didn't hesitate, despite the curve that Quin had just thrown him. Quin knew something, something that worried him enough that he intended to be visibly on the scene. The net was closing, the danger Killian had sensed rising. "That's not a problem. I like Silke's place better than this anyway."

Silke grimaced at the way Killian so blatantly announced their private arrangements. It wasn't that she was ashamed of their relationship, but she would have preferred a little more subtlety. "And I thought you were tactful."

Killian leaned back on his elbows, grinning at her disgruntled expression, realizing that she wasn't really irritated. "He's not exactly a hermit. I wanted to make sure he didn't get any ideas."

"You think that sounds better?" she demanded with lifted brows.

"No. But it's the truth."

Quin sighed, shaking his head. "My friend, you still haven't forgotten that pretty little Chinese girl. I promise you that I didn't know you had your eye on her. I can't help it that she thought I was more suited to her taste than you."

Silke laughed at the faint red that darkened Killian's tan. She hadn't thought she would ever see the day he looked remotely embarrassed. "This sounds like a good story." She folded her hands in her lap.

Killian shot her a lethal glare, adding a worse one for his tormentor. "How badly do you want that bed, Randy?"

Quin grimaced, his eyes suddenly hot. "Do you remember what I did to the last man who called me that?"

"You broke his nose."

"I haven't forgotten how."

"Silke wouldn't like it."

Silke tried not to giggle but didn't succeed. "I don't know. You might be even more interesting with a little crook in the middle."

Killian glared at her. "That's called tweaking the tail of the tiger."

Silke slithered off the bed, managing to keep her skirt at a respectable position while she got to her feet. "I tell you what. I'll go get Quin some wine while you two fight it out. And if I hear any thudding, I promise not to scream." She picked up her and Killian's empty glasses.

"Good idea," Killian agreed.

"Would you mind making mine tea?" Quin asked.

"We don't have any, I'm afraid. Would coffee do?"

"Killian's brand of acid?"

She shook her head. "No. Mine and it is drinkable. I promise."

He inclined his head, his light eyes holding appreciation he didn't verbally express. He watched her leave the room before turning back to Killian. "You have good taste."

"And we don't have much time. She'll be back in a few minutes. What have you got, and why do you want to stay so close?"

"There's a contract out on her. A nasty piece of work subbed out to a man who specializes in graphically visual hits. Big money. And your name's on the paper, too."

Killian's oath was rough, brutal, and crude.

Quin nodded again. "You're being watched at the office, but so far they haven't been able to track you here or get someone inside the personnel files. It seems that your secretary and that of the owner's younger brother have managed to misplace both of your records. A rather smooth move I thought."

Killian didn't acknowledge the compliment for one of his first countermoves. "Has the gun arrived in town?"

"Uncertain. My contacts are checking now."

"You can trust them not to sell us out?"

"You know better than that. I trust no one, but I pay better than anyone else and I don't cheat on my informers." He looked down at his scarred hands. "Besides, I don't deal kindly with disloyalty, especially not in this kind of a case."

Killian inclined his head as he studied Quin's set face. "You're making yourself a target as well. Divide and conquer."

Quin looked up, shrugging. "Still astute as ever."

You're crazy. You've got enough enemies who would pay more than whatever this bastard is paying for us."

Quin said nothing.

Killian looked into Quin's light eyes, adding the possibilities and not liking the tally. "Who is the hit man?"

Quin spoke the single name softly.

Killian's hands clenched into fists. Fear, not for himself, but for Silke, escalated beyond any that he had ever felt. "Top talent," he said finally, his voice rough with strain and frustration.

"Never caught. Never pictured. Never traced to any home base. A shadow out of a world filled with them." He turned his head to look over his shoulder. "You were right not to trust anyone else with her safety, you know. If she can be saved, we will do it better than anyone could. The law is bound hand and foot."

"And you're not."

His lips twisted cynically. "I know too much about too many very important people. And I know how to dodge very well."

Killian, too, looked toward the door through which Silke had passed. "One day you might want to settle. What then?"

"A very simple death for a man with too many enemies to ever live a peaceful life." His voice was whisper soft, final, peaceful.

Killian looked back at him. "How many times have you died?"

Quin blinked, startled at the question. The corners of his lips twitched, but he didn't smile. "I told you once we should have been partners."

"As I recall I was looking down the barrel of your gun at that particular moment, positive I was drawing my last few breaths."

"It didn't show."

"Good training."

"For both of us."

Killian cocked his head, hearing the sounds of Silke finishing in the kitchen. "You take this apartment tonight. Silke and I will stay in hers."

"Tomorrow we switch."

Killian inclined his head just before Silke entered with a mug of steaming coffee and their refilled wine glasses on a tray.

"Did I miss anything interesting?"

"No. Just us trading a few insults."

She nodded, her eyes gleaming with laughter. "Oh, male bonding."

Both men glared at the phrase. She plopped down on the bed, deciding that she liked Killian's friend very much. Only it would be nice if he smiled just once.

Killian eased his arm out from under Silke's head, being careful not to wake her. She had come to him so sweetly only hours before, pleasing him, taking him into her silken warmth as though he belonged to her and no other. But more importantly, she had fallen asleep in his arms as though she had never known the terror of her nightmares. Easing his pillows alongside of her, Killian slowly replaced his body with the inanimate objects, waiting to be certain that Silke didn't awake. When she only sighed in her sleep, curling close to the pillows that still bore his scent, he decided to risk slipping out of bed. He hated leaving her, but he had some details to work out with Quin. Without bothering to pull on any clothes, he walked into the living room to the wall both apartments shared. He tapped lightly, distinctly. Seconds spun into one minute, then his coded summons was answered. He nodded once, then went back for his jeans. He reached the front door of Silke's apartment as Quin knocked almost soundlessly. Neither man spoke until they reached the dark kitchen.

"I wish to hell you would see about getting some furniture if all you do is call some store and order the stuff," Quin murmured irritably. "I like a few luxuries. Even one chair would be nice."

"Forget the damn furniture. None of us is going to be here long enough to need it."

"The lady isn't staying? You surprise me. I didn't have her marked as a quitter."

"She isn't. The reasons she came never existed. And I don't intend to carry on this farce for any longer than it takes to guarantee her safety."

"She means that much to you?"

Until he heard the question voiced, Killian hadn't actually considered exactly how much he really did care for his golden-eyed seductress. "I love her," he said simply.

Quin listened to the tone, hearing the depth of need and astonishment without surprise. Killian, if he would but acknowledge it, was a man made for having a life partner. He wasn't built for being alone. "Have you told her?" he asked mildly.

"No!"

Quin's brows rose at the vehement negative. "Why not?"

"A little matter called trust. Silke has precious little reason to trust men or anyone who supposedly cares for her. With the exception of her adoptive family, she's been betrayed by everyone else." He paused, sighing deeply. "As I am betraying her now."

Silke leaned against the living room wall, stunned at the six words she had never thought to hear being spoken by Killian. She had awakened only moments before, alone in the bed. She hadn't been afraid. No nightmare had jerked her into alert tension. Rather, she had heard the nearby whisper of male voices. She had smiled as she had recognized Quin's and Killian's voices, although she couldn't make out the words. The friendship between the ill-matched pair still surprised her in some ways, yet it seemed as though only a man as unique as Killian was himself could appreciate him. She had risen from their bed, not really thinking about eavesdropping. She had simply wanted to share in that closeness as she had shared in it earlier in the evening.

But the closeness that included her was an illusion. The first words she had heard were Killian's damning announcement. Wrapping her arms around her body, curling deeper into the thick robe she had put on to join the men, she leaned against the wall and tried to get on top of the pain digging into her soul. As she waited, feeling her world burn around her, Killian lit other destructive fires.

"She thinks I came here by accident. Knowing about her reasons for leaving Philly wasn't unusual. There was a lot of gossip. She asked me once if I was following her. I told her yes and made it so that she wouldn't believe me. I told her the truth and cloaked it as a lie. Everything I did in those first few hours was with one purpose—to get close to her. I didn't like her when Geoffrey approached me with Lorraine's idea. I went to a party that she was attending, looking for some redeeming feature. I found what the papers reported so avidly. I judged her then. When part of my people went down with the flu, I took on Silke's pet guard dog assignment. I figured if I was going to have trouble it would be from her quarter. My firm's reputation is built on word of mouth as well as results. I didn't want one spoiled brat to mess up years of work."

Tears rained silently down Silke's face with every new revelation. If Killian had taken a sword and cut out her heart, he couldn't have done a better job of killing her. Feeling old, knowing she could stand no more truth this night, she pushed away from the wall and moved toward the kitchen. Her legs felt as though they didn't end in feet. Her breath was shallow, rough, uneven. But she moved, facing her living nightmare as she hadn't faced those that had driven her into the night. Her fingers found the light switch, flooding the small space with light.

Killian and Quin whirled around in individual, defensive stances. The light was cruel, highlighting the scene too vividly for anyone to miss the results of their midnight meeting. Killian took a step toward her.

Silke lifted her chin, her eyes blazing in a too pale face. "If you touch me, I will do my best to hurt you," she promised in a raw voice.

Killian stopped immediately. Every expression vanished from his face. The moment he had feared had come before he was ready, before the bridge of trust was strong enough to support what his lie would do. "How much did you hear?"

"I heard betrayal. Yours. My father's. My mother's. Tricks. Lies that were truths." Each answer was bitter agony, but she drove herself on. "I was easy, wasn't I?"

Killian's hands clenched into fists as he fought his need to demand she hear him. Only the agony he could see in her beautiful disillusioned eyes kept the slightest rein on his temper. "You were never easy."

She laughed harshly at that. "I don't know what you would call it then."

Quin shifted restlessly. "I'll leave you two alone." He started for the door.

Silke blocked him. "Take your friend with you when you go," she commanded.

He stopped before her, looking down at her face. "He won't go. And I can't make him."

"Won't." She didn't believe him.

"Can't. I should have finished the story about the night I held my gun on him. He took it away from me like a mother takes a toy from a child."

"Damn it, Quin. Shut up. You aren't helping."

Quin looked over his shoulder. "Neither are you by trying to spare her."

"Spare me?" Silke stared at both of them as though they had lost their minds. "Use me is more like it. Spy on me. Seduce me."

"You wanted me," Killian snapped back, stung into retaliating. "There was precious little seduction required."

Silke inhaled sharply, oddly unprepared for the thrust.

Killian swore a string of oaths, each more inventive than the last.

"Good move, Kill," Quin approved sarcastically.

"This isn't a damn game," Silke bit out.

Quin swung around, catching her shoulders. "No, it damn well isn't a game. I came halfway around the world, lady, to help someone I admire save your life. I don't care if he got you in bed at every opportunity. I do care that he doesn't want you dead, that your family doesn't want you dead. And while you're cursing him, you might want to know . . ." He got no farther.

Killian grabbed his arms, pulling him from Silke. "Shut up. I'll tell her what she needs to know. But not this way." He stepped between them, his body a human barrier of safety.

Quin glared at him. "You'll let her tear you into little pieces for her pride," he retaliated.

"My choice."

Silke heard the very real menace in their voices. Nothing made sense, and she wasn't even sure she wanted to find any more answers. The ones she had were bad enough. "Stop it, both of you," she said angrily.

Neither man even looked at her.

"She's stronger than you think."

"You don't know her at all."

Silke pushed hard on Killian's back. "Stop talking of me as if I were not here or making up fates for me just because my last name happens to be St. James. Contrary to my parents' opinion, I don't want or need your protection, Mr. Carpenter. And I sure don't want your lectures, Randall Quinlan. What I do want is for you both to go. And if I am very lucky, I won't ever see either of you again."

This time it was Killian who caught her, holding her even as she fought to be free of his touch. "I can't leave you."

"You'll get your money. I'll make sure my father knows how diligent you were at your job," she snapped, finally going limp in his hold.

Killian's eyes darkened at the bite of her rage. "I haven't any intentions of taking any money for being your guard dog or your lover. I don't need to be paid for either."

She tipped back her head, her eyes calling him a liar as she mutely stared back at him.

"Believe me or not as you choose. In the end it will be easy enough to prove." He turned her toward the bedroom. She balked.

"I'm not after your body and certainly not with an audience. I want your mind and you're going to let me have it."

"I will give you nothing."

Killian's lips tightened grimly, but he didn't stop their forward motion. If they were to have a future, it couldn't begin now. Instead, he concentrated on the present. Silke's life hung in the balance of an unforgiving god called greed.

"Get the lights, Quin," he said over his shoulder as he pushed Silke down on the bed they had shared so passionately. Her scent and his still lingered, but he hardly noticed. "If you try to, leave again, I'll tie you here until you listen to me," he added, making the words more a promise than a threat.

Silke glared at him, no longer lost in the fantasy he had given her. She read the hardness in the man she had thought she trusted. She believed him. Folding her hands in her lap, she tilted her chin and waited. If he wanted to spin tales, she would listen, but she wouldn't accept.

Killian analyzed her closed expression, seeing little of the woman he loved in her now. Her eyes were tiger gold and dangerous. Trust betrayed. He had known it would be bitter acid.

"You are in danger, and it has very little direct relation to who your parents are. If you believe nothing else tonight, believe that. That drug lord you were trying to nail has traced you here. There's a contract out on you. They mean to make your death very visual. It's a way of stopping any more loose tongues and frightening anyone thinking of getting out while the getting is good."

"Don't forget to tell her your name is right alongside of hers on that contract," Quin added dryly.

Killian didn't look his way. "Shut up, Quin."

Quin shrugged, then headed for the door. "I have a better idea. I'll leave you in here to sort this out, while I make us some coffee. We still have things to discuss."

Neither Killian nor Silke paid any attention to Quin's leaving. Silke stared at Killian, wondering if this were another trick. The dark look in his eyes, the tension in his body told the same story as his words. "Go on," she said slowly, not relaxing but listening.

"Originally, your father and mother contracted with me to provide four men to make certain that you and your sisters wouldn't be in any physical danger while you tried to find your feet in your new lives. They weren't supposed to have any personal contacts nor were they to report on your activities in any way unless you were physically at risk. I got involved because the company was hit hard with that damn flu epidemic. One of the original team was out and, quite simply, I didn't have anyone else to send but myself." He left out the part about his opinion of Silke and the trouble he had expected from her. She had already heard that one too many times. "Then your father came to me with this stalker tale he had concocted after you told him about what you had been doing. I had already seen you at that party by then. To protect you from the threat of an undetermined nature, I had to get close and there was no way you wouldn't remember if you happened to notice me trailing you around like an extra shadow. The only option left open was to get into your life on a friendly basis. I never planned to sleep with you."

Thirteen

Silke examined his words, looking for but not finding a single thing that she could fight. Everything he said made sense. But the knowledge did nothing to make her feel any less used, manipulated, moved about like a pawn on a chessboard. "You asked me for trust. I gave it."

Killian inclined his head, wishing he could touch her, reassure her and himself. "And you think I didn't give you the same in return?"

"I know you didn't," she replied flatly. "You could have told me when I told you about what I had been doing. It would have been the perfect opening."

Killian sat down beside her without touching her, ignoring the way she tensed. He held her gaze. "Would it have been, Silke? How would I have announced it? Oh, by the way, your father hired me to watch over you and created some cock-and-bull story about a stalker when all the time you've really had some drug supplier out combing the streets for you?" He didn't give her a chance to respond even if she had had the words. "I was angry when I realized that your father, my friend, had taken such a risk with your life. I was furious that you could be in a kind of danger that I hadn't known about and hadn't been guarding against. A stalker would have been wanting a more personal contact to make his move. A supplier might have been satisfied with shutting your beautiful mouth with something as simple as a high-powered rifle at long range." He grabbed her shoulders, the temper riding him as he shook her.

"Think, Silke. The choice was your life or living a damn lie. I chose the last and I damn well don't regret it. Hate me all you want, but that won't change what I did or how I feel about it."

Silke stared into his blazing eyes and read the truth that matched his words. He had asked her for trust. She had given him that and her body. One he had handled carefully, but the other he had abused. Her emotions demanded retaliation. She hurt all the way to her soul. She ached to lash out at him, her parents, the situation that held her life in a grip of pain, betrayed trust, and danger. She wanted to fight. She wanted to run. She wanted to wave a magic wand and find her lover waiting for her with desire in his eyes and truth on his lips. But reality couldn't be erased nor denied no matter how strong the wish. Nor could she walk away from the present that she had helped create. She hadn't needed Quin's comment to know that anyone close to her could share her risk. So she swallowed her pride, her hurt, her need to react. She slammed the lid on her emotions and turned the key in the lock.

Her logic, the part of her that had saved her life more than once, counseled a different reaction, a response based on facts. "I don't hate you. Right now, I have no feelings at all." If he hadn't been holding her, she would have missed the faint relaxation of tension in his big body. Before he could say or do anything, she continued hurriedly. "If I let myself feel, I might do something to you, my parents, or myself that I won't be able to make right. And I learned a long time ago, the worst thing to do is to make decisions in the heat of the moment." She reached up, wrapped her fingers around his wrists, and pulled his hands from her shoulders. She would make herself survive having him in her life for as long as it took, but no amount of emotional control would outweigh the seduction of his touch and the memories that each whisper of his scent invoked. "I've learned a lot about myself over the years. I'm a survivor. I won't try to send you away. I won't knowingly do anything to make this situation more difficult for any of us. I don't want anyone's death on my conscience. So I'll play this game out to the end. But I will not be your friend. I will not let you touch me. I will not want you."

Killian looked into those eyes that boiled with emotions barely held in check and knew that he had never loved or admired Silke more. He could have told her it wasn't over between them. He could have told her that he loved her, since it was clear she hadn't heard that part of his and Quin's discussion earlier. But the time wasn't right. And the risk was no different now than it had been all along. His choices were dictated by his need to keep her safe. He didn't dare push her with one more truth that she could be forgiven for believing was a lie.

"All right. No sex. If that is the condition for my presence, then so be it."

After nodding once, Silke rose and went to the closet. "Quin said something about plans. If we are going to have a council meeting, I'm getting dressed."

Killian got to his feet. "Good idea." He headed for the door, pausing with his back to her. "Silke?"

Silke glanced over her shoulder, frowning at his position. "Yes?"

"Thank you for the decision you made. I know it wasn't easy. I would have hated having to force you to accept me."

She allowed herself a small smile at the understatement. "Maybe that's why I didn't fight it or you."

Killian almost smiled at the response. She was coming back from the blow his betrayal had dealt her. It was enough for now. "I always knew you were a smart lady." He opened the door and left the room, shutting the panel soundlessly behind him.

Silke's shoulders slumped tiredly as she stared at the clothes in the closet. Her vision blurred. She dabbed at her eyes with the corner of her robe, angry at the tears that wouldn't stop. She wasn't one of those women who cried superbly, and she didn't want Killian to know how much he had hurt her. She wasn't strong enough to see the knowledge in his eyes. She lifted her chin. She hadn't been de-feated yet. And she wouldn't be. Not by the situation or the man.

Killian rubbed his neck wearily as he entered the kitchen. Quin turned, looking him over carefully.

"She didn't handle it well?"

"She handled it better than any of us had a right to expect. She's going to let us stay, and she has promised to cooperate completely."

Quin's brows rose in surprise. "Smart lady. Gutsy."

Killian reached for the coffeepot and a mug, pouring himself a cup before he answered. "She's that and more. Damn, I hate hurting her!" he exploded with muted violence. "I don't know how she's doing it, but she locked herself away somehow. One second I thought she would rage out her pain, slice me to ribbons if she could. She looked at me with those tiger eyes, and I knew she would have taken my heart roasted over a flame if she could. I wanted that fight."

Quin's hands tightened around his own mug, reading the agony that lay in each word and understanding Killian's need for the air-clearing confrontation. "But she didn't fight. She won and she probably doesn't even know she chose the one tactic against which you would have no defense." He looked past Killian's face to the empty living room. "What is she doing right now?"

"Dressing for our discussion," Killian said flatly before he took another swallow of coffee.

"How much are you going to tell her?"

Killian didn't hesitate. "Everything. It's her life, and there isn't one reason she shouldn't know."

Silke walked into the room in time to hear the last words. "At least that's a change," she murmured, walking past Killian without touching him, a difficult feat to make look natural in the narrow confines of the kitchen.

She glanced at Quin more to avoid looking at Killian than for any other reason. An instant later she wished she had chosen a wall or any inanimate object. The knowing look in the other man's eyes recognized her strategy. Her chin tilted in defiance and chal-lenge. That smile that wasn't a smile at all touched the corners of his mouth before he took the last mug on the counter and filled it. He handed it to her.

"I'd better warn you. I make lousy coffee."

Silke took a sip and grimaced. "You're right. You do."

Killian glared at the two of them. Whatever emotions Silke was holding in check obviously didn't extend to Quin. "Now that we've established that earth-shattering fact, could we get to the plans?" he asked, setting his cup on the counter.

"I have a better question. Where would you like us to do this planning?" Quin murmured, amused at Killian's expression. He had never known the man to be less than formidable in his ability to handle himself. But he wasn't succeeding this time, and Quin didn't have far to look for the reason. It stood right in front of him, trying to look and feel completely unmoved by the raging male behind her. Not that that was working any better than Killian's attempt at composure. Her eyes were betraying her almost as much as Killian's temper. "Shall we adjourn to the bedroom? At least we can all sit down there."

"No!"

"No!"

Silke swung around to glare at Killian.

He glared back.

Quin shook his head. Carrying his mug, he strolled between them and headed for the bedroom. "I'm too damn tired to argue or stand when I could be sitting. And since I know Killian doesn't go in for spectator bedroom sports and you, Silke, have too much class to agree anyway, I'm not worried about being embarrassed."

Silke hadn't thought she could blush. She discovered she was wrong in listening to that dark voice murmur his outrageous comment. Killian swore. Silke's blush and Quin's words were tinder to his temper.

"One more word, Quin," he warned, following the taller man.

Quin put his cup on the windowsill, glanced once at Killian's set face, and decided he had prodded him enough to get rid of the worst of his temper. "Get the other side of the comforter."

Silke brushed past Killian, not wanting him handling the bed linen at all. "I'll do it."

In seconds she and Quin had smoothed the bed, and the three

of them took their places, neither she nor Killian close enough to touch accidentally.

Killian had never felt less like figuring a strategy, but he made himself concentrate on the logistics of keeping Silke alive. "I think the best plan is for me to stick to Silke and to restrict our time out in the open. There is no sense in giving our man a free shot at her. But, we also don't want to go completely underground either. Right now, we know that there is one person out there waiting for us. I'd like to use that to our advantage, draw him in to us rather than the other way. If we plan it right, we can catch the gunman here at the same time the law moves in on the supplier at home. If we miss the timing, then we very well could be dealing with more than one contract."

Silke considered his plan, finding it risky but the best possible chance in the circumstances, assuming they stayed in Atlanta. "We could go back to Philly," Silke suggested without looking at him.

Killian stared at her averted face for a moment, already feeling the pinch of how she avoided any and all contact with him. He hadn't missed the change in her expression when she thought he was going to touch the bed they had shared. He could have told her he had no more need to torture himself with what had been than she did.

"Then we're on his home turf. At least here, he's not so certain who we know or just how much we can do," Killian replied as neutrally as he could manage. "But I will escort you back if you really want to go."

Killian's offer surprised her, but she didn't let either man see. She had finished giving away her secrets. "No. I was hoping you wouldn't suggest that. I've been worried about my parents and my sisters. If he can't get me, he might try for them."

"He could," Killian agreed, hating giving her this truth but determined there would be nothing but honesty between them now. "I don't think he will. But we are taking precautions in case I'm wrong. The three men watching your sisters have been notified, and I have sent two more to each as backup and round-the-clock guards. As for your parents, they've got the same setup."

Silke looked at Quin. "What's your role? You said you came halfway around the world to help Killian. But specifically to do what?"

"Gather information, mostly." Quin glanced at Killian, his light brows raised as he asked the silent question. "Killian's determined to be your shadow. With him chained to you, he can't go hunting and he doesn't want to trust too many people he doesn't know."

"Tell her everything. No more secrets."

Quin sighed deeply. "I was afraid you would say that." He looked at Silke, seeing the confusion she wasn't quick enough to hide in her eyes. "I'm not exactly what you would term respectable. In fact, in some circles, I'm considered dishonest, even criminal."

Silke frowned. Somehow the image didn't quite fit the man, although some instinct told her it wouldn't have been social rules that would have dictated Quin's choices but a code of honor uniquely his own. Like Killian's, a small voice whispered. Although very opposite in looks, the two men had a lot in common.

"So you can move in and around the dark areas with less ripples than Killian would cause if he were to try, " she said finally.

Quin's eyes flickered with surprise and increasing admiration. "Something like that." He also could have added he was not as nice in his choices as Killian, but that knowledge wouldn't have done anything to reassure this strange woman who could accept darkness and light with equal calm. Killian had chosen very well indeed, and if Quin could help these two come together, he would do so for the sake of his friend and the debt he owed, as well for the admiration he was coming to feel for this unusual woman.

"And information is power," Silke murmured.

"And in our case, it is also the best chance we have for countering the gun sent to get you," Killian inserted bluntly.

Silke looked at Killian directly for the first time since they had sat down on the bed. She hadn't forgotten what Quin had said about the contract for her death. "Get us."

Killian studied her, seeing concern where there had only been betrayal lurking in her eyes. Suddenly, the darkness that had surrounded him when she had learned the beginning of his role in her life wasn't so very black after all. She couldn't care what happened to him and hate him at the same time.

"Get us," he agreed slowly, deeply.

* * *

Silke met his gaze, feeling his warmth seep into the cold that had come with the words she had overheard. She tried to resist the feeling, the softening she could detect stealing past her mental barriers to her heart.

"I don't want anyone hurt on my account."

Killian almost smiled at her belligerence. "Did I say otherwise?"

Silke scowled.

Quin shook his head and wondered if Killian had a death wish. This lady was definitely not the type to tease, especially when she was a breath away from open mayhem. "Anyone have anything to add to the master plan?" he asked.

Killian glanced at his friend, recognizing the diversion. "Nothing more than make sure you stay alive."

"Let's make sure we all stay alive," Silke murmured vehemently.

Quin got to his feet with a nod. "Now that's settled, I intend to get some sleep. You probably won't see me leave tomorrow, or rather later this morning. I'll report in when I have something." He collected their empty mugs and took them with him when he left.

Killian acknowledged his going with an inclination of his head, but his eyes never left Silke's face. He said nothing as he listened for the outer door to close. There was one truth remaining. He didn't expect her to believe him, but he had made a promise and he intended to keep it.

Silke shifted restlessly as Killian continued to look at her without moving. She wanted to get up, to ask him to leave. Both would have betrayed how much his steady regard unnerved her and that she couldn't allow. So she faced him, holding his gaze, waiting. But when the waiting was suddenly terminated in three soft words, she froze, every nerve, every sinew rejecting what he said.

"I love you. I know you don't want to believe me," Killian said quietly. "You can hate me if you want. You can try to run if you can. You can tell me you don't believe me. But nothing is going to change the truth."

Silke surged to her feet, too tempted to stay on the bed, too tempted to let herself be lulled into accepting the words at face value. "Truth is a matter of perception."

He nodded, watching her pace, feeling her need to deny him

as a pain almost as great as that of the moment in the kitchen when he had seen the betrayal bloom in her eyes. "Yes. It is also a matter of fact, undeniable, inescapable, relentless, and demanding." He rose then, going to stand in front of her without touching her.

Silke stopped a pace away, her head tilting back so that she could analyze his expression. What she saw reflected there shocked any rebuttal she might have made right out of her. Naked need, undisguised, glowed in his eyes. Sincerity that couldn't be questioned reinforced the emotion, defining and highlighting it. She breathed deeply, caught when she would rather have been free.

"I don't need pretty words," she said finally. "You gave me pleasure. I can accept that. Live with it."

Killian halved the distance between them but still didn't touch her. "I gave you love."

She shook her head, wanting more than her next breath to have the strength to move away from him. "Pleasure."

He raised his hand slowly, watching her eyes follow every move he made. He expected her to flinch, at least to dodge his touch. Instead, she looked straight at him, her gaze questioning, wary, and strangely vulnerable. His fingers settled lightly on her cheek, stroking gently down the elegant curve to her chin. He cupped it, looking at her mouth, remembering her taste.

Silke stood imprisoned by his hold, yet knowing that all she had to do was take a step back and she would be free. But would she? she wondered silently as he moved closer so that his body brushed her as lightly, as delicately as his forefinger traced her lips. She shivered, feeling as though she were perched on the edge of a dark abyss, where one tiny change in balance would send her either reeling into the blackness, alone and lost, or falling back into the warmth of arms that had known her, cared for her, waited for her.

"If this is a lie," she whispered, forcing the words past his tantalizing touch, "it would be kinder to let the gunman coming to kill me win."

Killian slipped his free hand around her neck, his thumb at the base of her throat. A little pressure and her face was just at the right angle. "No lie, Silke." He searched her eyes. Tenderness. A new emotion so alien to him that he found it was a kind of pleasure just to explore the range of feeling that came with each touch. "You don't have to love me back either."

Her brows rose at the quiet statement. "I don't?" she asked, feeling the attraction of the abyss and the warmth that lay around her, promising her a life of safety and caring. Either choice required courage, different kinds perhaps, but nerve to match anything she had ever done.

Killian bent his head, his lips replacing his finger to trace the outline of her mouth. "No, you don't. Come to me for pleasure if that is all I can give you. But come to me . . ." He kissed her tenderly, cherishing her mouth as he had cherished and loved her body. "Please."

One word. A simple courtesy that wrapped around her like a silver thread, drawing her steadily back from the abyss to the haven of the warmth. It was Killian, the heat of his body mating with hers, the fire in his desire to warm the night and burn away the nightmares so that the healing balm of sleep awaited her with the ending of each day. Her arms rose, slipping around him, holding him as she had been afraid to do since she had heard those words of apparent betrayal.

"I don't know what I feel," she whispered against his mouth, her eyes shutting as the sting of tears surprised her. "I want to be with you, hold you, find pleasure with you in the night." She drew back to look at him, not trying to hide the confusion she felt. "That seems a poor exchange for love."

He smiled faintly, relaxing as he hadn't since she had turned from him, her eyes filled with the agony he had brought with his caring. "If I am satisfied, then you should be as well. Besides, who knows what the future holds? One morning you may wake beside me and think of love and me."

"You'd take that chance on me?" No one, not even the parents she had come to love, had ever offered to run such a risk for her sake. Awed and frightened, she wanted to shake him, to ask if he understood the concept of self-preservation.

"All of life is a chance. You, of all the people I know, must realize that."

She shook her head. "It's not fair."

His smile widened, reaching to his eyes, glittering with a challenge that he hoped she couldn't resist. "Then give me more."

She shook her head, trying to draw away but finding she was bound now by his arms, caged by the strength of his body. "I don't know if I can."

"Don't you want to find out? Do you really want an affair with me, a limited time that will end someday? Is that enough for a woman who has been a virgin in an era and from a background where being untouched was as unique as the Immaculate Conception?"

Silke froze. Truth stole her need to run. Truth held her with more strength than any human, even one as powerful as Killian, could match. Love. The Grail. The goal. The impossible wish on a star. Hers if she was brave enough to reach for that glittering constellation, brave enough to survive the fire of passion, brave enough to listen to her heart and forget all the reasons she knew that betrayal and pain lurked in those four letters. In that moment, she learned something about herself. No matter what her adoptive family had done or been, she had always kept one part of herself free, aloof from that final commitment. That was why she had not told her family what she had been doing, why she allowed them to believe, as the world believed, in her wild ways.

"Don't do this to me," she murmured, her throat tight against the need to weep. Tears ran down her face but she didn't feel them.

Killian pulled her close, tucking her head close to his heart. "Don't, Silke. Scream, hurl abuse at my head, but don't cry."

She buried her face against him, hearing his heart as gentle thunder beneath her ear. "I can't stop."

Lifting her in his arms, he carried her to their bed, coming down beside her, holding her as the flood continued, growing stronger, more demanding of her slender body. He leaned his cheek against her hair, hating the emotion tearing her apart but knowing that, somehow, this outpouring had to occur for any future to exist for either of them. Minutes were measured in her tears, the catches in her throat as she tried to fight her emotions. He ached for her, with her, every inch of the way. And then finally, she lay spent and silent beside him, her arms tight around his neck, his shirt damp with the pain she had suffered before he had even entered her life. He didn't need the words to understand the fight going on within her. He didn't know if he would win, if the hold of the past was weaker than the promise of the future. What he did know was that he would be there for her whatever choice she made.

Fourteen

The man stared across the street at the building that was the new home of Douglas Plastics. He hadn't caught a glimpse of Silke Brown-St. James since she had arrived for work with Killian Carpenter. Both were still in the building. Not that it mattered. They could enjoy their few days of freedom. In the end he would have both of them. The payoff was the largest he had ever negotiated. Greed rode him hard, demanding action. But experience had taught valuable lessons in patience. He would wait, learn his quarries, plan his hit. The boss wanted it high profile. He licked his lips in anticipation. That was a bonus, one he intended to enjoy as he enjoyed few things but money. Suddenly, he caught a movement at the back entrance. He glanced at his watch, a thin smile distorting the smooth, almost gentle lines of his face. If he had stood in a police lineup, no one would have taken him for one of the most notorious hitmen in the country.

"Come to me, pretty little Silke doll," he crooned, watching as Silke stepped out into the late afternoon sun. Light caught like trapped fire in her hair. He had always liked redheads with their hot tempers. The man Killian was right beside her, scanning the area, looking for him. "But you won't find me, smart man. No one has. No one will. You'll see me only when you are counting your last seconds and listening to your woman scream hers. Then you'll know me. You'll carry my face with you into hell."

Killian shifted his shoulders, feeling the hairs on the back of his neck stand on end. They were being watched. He didn't need to see their audience to know it existed.

"He's here, isn't he?" Silke murmured as she matched Killian's fast pace to the garage.

"Yes." Killian gave her a swift glance, seeing that she was just as alert as he, just as on guard for anything.

"I think I'm glad he wants to make an example of me. We both might be dead right now," she added bluntly.

He nodded as he returned to his visual sweep of the area, the possible vantage points that only an army of men would have been able to cover. A second later they entered the relative shelter of the garage. He felt rather than heard the slight expulsion of breath that showed Silke was aware of how at risk they were in the open. Despite the supposed terms of the hit, the gun might just decide to make his money the easy way.

"How long do you think it will take Quin to come up with something? If he can come up with something in an area where he doesn't normally work."

"I wish I knew," he replied honestly. Killian stopped beside the car without touching it and took out a small device that could detect certain kinds of bombs. First, he checked the car for any obvious signs of tampering, not that he expected a professional to leave any marks for him to find. Then before he used the high-tech gadget he had carried in a special pocket in his jacket. As he suspected, there was nothing unusual under the hood, the seats, wired to the door locks, ignition, or under the chassis.

"All right," he said, opening the passenger door for her.

Silke settled into the seat, exhaling tiredly. She hadn't realized how difficult today was going to be. Not that this was the last of the hours of sitting on a powder keg. As she watched Killian walk around to his side of the car, she thought of the night before, of crying in his arms, of falling asleep the same way. He hadn't made love to her, not then or in the morning when he had wakened her with a touch of his lips to hers. He had smiled at her, asking nothing but a smile in return.

"Stop worrying," Killian said, glancing at her before he put the key in the ignition.

"I wasn't."

"You're sure? You looked it."

"Why didn't you make love to me last night or this morning?" she asked before she thought.

His hand stilled just as he started to turn on the engine. He faced her slowly, his gaze as startled as it was curious. "You think I would have taken advantage of you last night or this morning?"

She frowned at the neutral sound of his voice. Although she couldn't hear any anger, she could feel it, waves of it filling the car. "I didn't think of it like that."

"Well, I would have. I love you. I don't want you weak beneath me, giving in because I caught you with your guard down. Even if I didn't love you, I wouldn't want you that way. No real man would."

Silke thought that over, finding another facet to this man when she had thought she knew enough. She also discovered that she would have, for once in her life, preferred to have had the decision made for her. "It would have been easier."

"Less honest. And in the end, it would have cost too much for both of us."

"Yes," she agreed with a sigh.

He stroked her cheek lightly. "Stop worrying. Everything will work out."

"Since when did you start being an optimist?" She leaned into his touch, smiling faintly.

"I'd rather hope than drag my tail around in defeat." He laughed softly at her expression. "And so would you."

She shrugged and pulled back slowly so that he was no longer touching her. "I might just change my tactics in life if this mess is any indication of what I have to look forward to," she replied, changing the subject. She wasn't ready to come face to face with their future. But she didn't want to hurt Killian by telling him so.

Killian wondered if she knew how revealing her expression was since she had become his lover. The games she had played and might well play again had been roles so perfect he hadn't had a real clue about the woman beneath. Now, he did know her, had possessed and been possessed by her. The veils under which she had hidden herself had disappeared as early morning mist before the sun. He turned and started the car.

"You'd make the same choices again. And again. That's your nature, just as it is mine."

Silke leaned back in her seat, no longer surprised at how well he read her. In some ways, she was even coming to depend on his ability to see beneath the surface. It gave her a measure of security that she hadn't been aware of needing. She sighed gently, accepting what she would have fought not so long ago. She glanced at him, seeing his concentration on the traffic. Killian was safety, a haven in so many ways. But more, he asked nothing of her that she couldn't give. He was completion. And she wanted him and what he brought to her. She wanted, also, to give. The question was whether she would have enough to hold him, to build a future, or whether the past had scarred her so deeply that nothing could erase the wounds, the taint of what she had been and done.

The man followed carefully, keeping different cars between himself and his quarry. He frowned as he realized that Carpenter was making no attempt to lose any tail. His eyes narrowed as he considered the implications of this behavior. A trap? Perhaps, but he had always escaped before. The traffic thinned slightly as they moved farther from the center of the business and commercial district, and still Carpenter showed no inclination to avoid any tail. The man slipped even farther back in traffic, his greed strong but his survival instinct stronger. He almost missed the turnoff they made into the small apartment complex. He had to backtrack and by then he had lost them. Cursing, he eased down the streets between the quads, looking for Killian's car. Finally, he had just about decided that Carpenter had outsmarted him after all, when he saw it parked in front of one of the four units.

"Gotcha now, smart man," he muttered, going by as though he didn't have any interest in anything in the area.

"Did he stop?" Silke asked, standing slightly behind Killian, shielded by him from the window beside which they both stood.

Killian shook his head without taking his eyes from the non-descript car that was making a turn in the cul-de-sac at the end of the street. He couldn't see the driver, but he did have the license number, not that it would be much use if it was, as he suspected, a rental car. It was unlikely that the man would have given his real name to the agency.

"I still don't see the logic in letting him follow us here."

Killian released the slat in the mini-blind and moved toward the bed to sit down. "I'm trying to speed this up for one thing. And to get our man out in the open. If he thinks he might have a shot, not literally, at you, it is less likely he'll start thinking in terms of long-range-type hits."

Silke sat down beside him. "We're dangling the bait a little."

He met her gaze without flinching. "You were that before I ever entered the picture. I'm just using it to our advantage instead of letting it be used against you."

She thought that over. Had she been a woman who quailed at unpalatable facts she would have been hurt at his attitude. But she believed in reality being better than false illusions and promises. "What can I do to help?" she asked finally.

His lips curved slightly at her determined expression. "Do the impossible. Look accessible while you're wearing a full suit of armor and guarded by an army."

She laughed, finding it surprisingly easy to do as she sat beside him on the bed, feeling the life coursing through him, the need sizzling in her own body. Death might await her in the shadows, but right now she thought only of life and passion. She leaned toward him, her eyes glittering with desire. This time her decision was easy.

"Make love to me."

Killian heard and read her need. His body tightened in immediate response. He caged the awakening beast for one moment. "Why?"

"Because I want you."

"Pleasure?" Even he could hear the sudden flatness of his voice.

She shook her head. "More." She cupped his jaw, her fingers just touching the corner of his mouth. She stared at the full curves that could breathe fire on her skin, drive her out of her mind with wanting. "Just don't ask me for names or labels. I'm not that brave yet." She looked up, holding his gaze. "I want to be but I'm not." She felt the cost of the admission to her soul. She had never felt so stripped of defenses. One word from him could destroy her or give her a path into the future. Tense, she waited for his answer.

Killian released the breath he hadn't been aware of holding. It was more than he had expected. He leaned closer, bending his head so that his mouth hovered only a kiss away. "All right. No labels." His name touched his mouth before her kiss. A benediction, a plea, a demand. He didn't know. And in that moment, he didn't care.

* * *

Quin stretched his shoulders tiredly as he eased out of the rental car to step into the coolness of the early Georgia evening. Killian's apartment was across the common. Around it were empty parking places. But he had chosen this place. No one would look here for an extra car that might betray his presence in the apartment. He scanned the area as he made his way across the green. No one looked suspicious although there were a number of people coming and going. But no matter how innocent the scene looked, he had a feeling that one Eric Lane had managed to find Killian and Silke. He smiled grimly to himself. The man would have been better served if he had taken his money and run. Killian would let no one harm the woman he had finally named as his mate. Eric would not touch Silke as long as Killian lived. If Quin knew one thing in life, it was the strength of the one man in the universe he truly respected and came as close to liking as it was possible for him to get.

He mounted the stairs, staying in the shadows that were, at this moment, more friend than foe. Killian's apartment was dark inside. No light spilled into the night to betray the fact that he had opened the door just enough for his body to slide in. He walked to the common wall between the apartments, tapping on the end that would sound softly in Silke's bedroom. A second later one knock signaled he would soon have company. Stripping off his coat, he tossed it on the made bed and wandered into the kitchen.

"So Quin came back tonight after all. Whoever our contract man is, he must be easier to find than you led me to believe," Silke murmured quietly as she slipped into a pair of jeans and a silk shirt.

Killian zipped up his dress slacks, part of the same outfit he had worn to work. "He probably wasn't easy at all. Quin just has a knack for getting blood out of stone when it's necessary."

"Probably because he looks so damn dangerous," she agreed, following him out of the bedroom into the empty living room. She glanced around. "You know he's right. We should get some furniture. When this is over that's going to be one of my top priorities even if I have to shop at the thrift stores to do it."

Killian stopped at the door, turned, and wrapped his hand

around the back of her neck. He hauled her close and kissed her
hard. "You won't have to shop at thrift stores and you won't be
staying here," he said roughly. "We're going home when this mess
is cleared up. Whatever your sisters have or have not done with
their lives, you have been doing something with yours. You don't
need to prove yourself anymore."

Silke drew back, shocked at the depth of knowledge, of certainty in his voice. "Do you mean that?"

"The only things I mean more are that I love you and I'm
going to protect you with every trick I know and any I need to
make up along the way." He brushed a strand of red hair back
behind her ear. "I'm going to be your shadow."

She smiled, feeling curiously free with the promise of his continued presence regardless of how uncertain she had been. "And
I'm going to let you."

He laughed, kissing her once more. "Do you really think I
would let you stop me?"

"Yes. You told me so and I believed you," she replied the minute he released her lips enough so that she could speak. "I trust
you to be telling me the truth."

Killian stared into her extraordinary eyes and knew that he was
slowly gaining ground over the damage of her past. With every
breath she drew, Silke was coming closer to the final commitment.
Pride in her, in the woman she had become out of the ashes of the
child she had been, filled him. His eyes glowed with it. He wanted
to tell her what he felt, but he dammed the words unspoken. The
decision would come on its own and in its own time. That was as it
should be and the only way in which he wanted it.

He took her hand. "Come on. Quin will be wondering what happened to us." He stepped out of the apartment, checking the area
before he allowed Silke to follow, keeping himself between Silke
and the open balcony. For a bullet to reach her soft body, it had to
pass through his first. But there was no bullet, nothing in the darkness but the gentle fragrance of the night flowers, the muted sounds
of a world settling itself for sleep. Killian didn't relax. With every
minute that flowed through the hourglass of universal time he had
that much more to lose. He tapped once on the door.

Quin opened it a crack before Killian could remove his fingers
from the wood. He waited only the time it took for both to enter

before shutting it again. Only then did he reach for the light switch.

"Well," Killian demanded impatiently.

"He's here."

"I thought so. We were followed coming in tonight. I got the license. The car was rented to an Adam Macon."

"Imaginative." Quin headed for the kitchen, opening the refrigerator. "I don't know about you two, but I'm hungry."

Killian ignored the reference to Quin's appetite. When Quin was at his most vague was when his mind was in high gear. "What else did you get?"

"The man has developed a recent liking for knives. Makes his own in fact, and he prides himself on killing his victims slowly with the maximum amount of discomfort."

Silke shuddered. "Nice," she muttered.

Quin glanced over his shoulder, smiling that not quite smile. "Actually it is. Professional arrogance is one of the flaws that can kill a man. And to waste someone slowly requires two very important factors. Time and privacy. That's how we're going to bag this villain." He returned his attention to the contents of the refrigerator, finally selecting a carton of eggs, ham, cheese, bread, potatoes, and tomatoes. "I found out where he's staying. Not that it will do us much good. No privacy for one thing and, for another, this rat never takes his prey to his lair."

"You've been busy," Killian murmured, doing some high-speed thinking of his own.

Quin rolled up his sleeves without looking around. "How do you want to play it? Bait and trap?"

Killian looked at Silke, seeing not the unmarred perfection of her form but what she could be if they didn't succeed, plan or no plan. "I don't want to."

Quin shrugged, his attention squarely on the eggs he was whisking to a froth. If she were his woman, if he had a woman to call his own, he wouldn't want to make the choice that lay in Killian's hands. No matter how good he and Killian were, there were variables that couldn't be anticipated. Those variables had killed more good men than the world would ever count.

"Don't I get a vote in this?" Silke asked when she finally realized that Killian wasn't going to ask her to make this choice.

"You get a vote all right, but first, we have to decide if we have any kind of shot at keeping you alive if you decide to be the bait." Killian studied her, for the first time in a long while able to look past the woman he loved to the female strong enough to fight for her own life if it became necessary.

"I have faith in you," she said quietly. "If there is any way to keep me safe, I know you will find it." She glanced at Quin. "And you, too," she added.

Quin's not quite smile flashed as he looked over his shoulder. "It's nice to be remembered."

Killian felt her vote of confidence to the darkest corners of his mind. He had her trust, more perhaps than he deserved. "Can you shoot a gun?"

Surprised at the abrupt question, Silke looked back at him. "After a fashion. Aim for the belly, hold it steady, and squeeze the trigger."

Killian's lips twisted at the description. "That will do." He looked at Quin. "You did get me what I asked."

Quin inclined his head toward the drawer closest to Killian. "It's in there."

Killian opened it and pulled out a small, dark automatic. It fit comfortably in the palm of his hand, a toy that wasn't a toy at all. He handed it to Silke, watching as she checked the safety then the clip. "You'll do."

She smiled faintly. "Only because I have to. I really hate these things. But I like being dead even less."

Quin laughed, surprising them all. "I knew you were one gutsy lady," he murmured, tipping out the first perfectly cooked omelet into a plate he had warming in the oven.

"I do my poor best," she agreed, amazed that there was anything funny at this moment. She glanced back at the gun she held. "This should fit into my handbag with no trouble."

"No."

She looked up at Killian. "What do you mean no?"

"I mean it's too damn easy for you to get separated from the bag. I want this thing on you." He pulled a slender harness from the drawer and held it out to her. "You're going to wear it."

"Won't he search me if you don't get him before he gets me?"

"He could. The odds are he won't."

Quin tipped out the second omelet. "It's the best shot you're going to get," he said, adding his weight to the argument.

Silke thought that over as she tested the weight of the gun in her hand. "All right," she said finally, repressing a shiver as she imagined the feel of the cold metal that could spell death touching her skin. She believed too passionately in life to be comfortable with what the morning might bring.

Killian caught the emotions chasing across her face, accurately interpreting them. He closed the distance between them to cup her chin with one hand. "If you can't do it, Silke, if you can't aim that thing and pull the trigger knowing you might kill this man who would kill you, tell us now."

She met his eyes. "And you'll do what? Take me out of this? You know it has gone beyond that. We have to stop it here or more will come. And every time I'm a target there is that much more chance an innocent might get in the way, maybe someone I love or maybe just a stranger. But someone will pay the price for my choices. I can't live with that."

"Can you live with what you might have to do to protect yourself?" He had to be sure. Her life depended on him, Quin, and her own courage to help herself if they couldn't.

"I've lived with worse and survived," she replied simply, her hand reaching up to touch his cheek, her warmth comfort against what might happen to any of them. She couldn't change the past, rewrite the present, or even walk away from the future. She could only stand beside this man who loved her and the friend he had brought to help save her life.

Killian turned his face so that his lips kissed the heart of her palm. His eyes softened for a moment, the hard purpose of a difficult course fading briefly from his gaze. "I'm counting on that survival instinct of yours. Make sure it doesn't let you down or I'll follow you into eternity."

Silke laughed softly, pleased at the threat, oddly reassured when she hadn't known she needed to be. "I'll remember that," she promised.

Quin slid the last omelet onto the plate. "Now that we have that settled, let's eat. I'm starving."

Killian released Silke, stepping back when he would rather have drawn her into his arms. For the first time since he had called Quin, he wished him a hundred miles away.

Quin shot him a perceptive look, his eyes glittering with amusement. If a man could choke on frustration, Killian was giving a good imitation. "Stop glaring at me. Another hour and you'll have her all to yourself." He thrust a plate at him. "Find your own drink. I'm having coffee." He picked up his mug and plate and left the kitchen.

Silke bit her lip to keep from giving way to the humor of watching Quin watch Killian. "When this is over, you have to tell me how you two ended up being friends."

Killian scowled even though he was delighted with the reference to the future he wasn't positive existed for them. "I don't know if we are friends." He reached into the refrigerator and pulled out a bottle of wine. Silke shook her head when he offered to pour her a glass. "Allies comes closer to the mark. I don't think Quin will ever trust anyone enough to really be friends." He collected his plate and glass, waiting until Silke poured herself a cup of coffee to go with her meal. Together they followed Quin to the bedroom to find him settled on one corner of the bed, his plate balanced perfectly on his knees. "Are we friends, Quin?" Killian asked as he sat down.

Quin's light brows raised at the question. "Hardly," he returned dryly. "Associates, perhaps. Why?"

"I asked."

"The curiosity of a woman. Always wanting labels." There was amusement in his pale eyes, a wealth of cynicism and disillusionment.

"And yet you came when he called."

"Killian would have for me."

"And that isn't friendship?"

He shook his head. "There are too many loopholes in friendship to fit us. Therefore, no friendship exists." He sighed when she looked confused. "We share a debt. His. Mine. A bond better and more dependable than emotion. Honor. His. Mine. Easier to define. Tangible. Not open for interpretation."

"Safe," she murmured, beginning to understand. Caprice and she shared such a debt, a bond. And it definitely was stronger than friendship. Safer.

Quin inclined his head, making no effort to deny the word. "Safe." He returned his attention to his food. "You have one of those bonds?"

"My sister."

He looked up, searching her face, then Killian's. "You didn't tell me she had a sister."

"I didn't know it was important."

He shrugged. "Perhaps not."

Silke looked from one to the other, suddenly feeling as though she had stumbled into a minefield of unanswered questions. She opened her mouth to ask, but the faint shake of Killian's head stopped her. When Killian changed the subject without warning, she followed his lead, the questions still in her mind. Something else to ask Killian when they were free of the shadow hanging over them.

Fifteen

"Will you relax, Kill? The plan is the best we can do. The police have the garage tied down. You'll be in there when Eric makes his move and I'll be outside with a high-powered rifle as insurance if something goes wrong."

"I don't like it. Eric moved in on her too damn fast. I don't want to find out our trap is really his."

"I told you the kind of money the man is getting. And you know what Geoffrey told you. The supplier has a time limit in days even if he doesn't know the sting is set for today. Eric just doesn't have the hours to play it safe. Besides, as far as he knows, you and Silke are so busy rolling in the sheets you don't know you're in danger."

Killian shifted restlessly, staring beyond Quin to the man across the street they had been watching for hours. Eric had followed Silke to work and parked across the street, where he had a view of the garage and the back entrance to Douglas Plastics. He had wandered the area, seeming to have business in a couple of the buildings, when in reality he was checking the place out. Suddenly, Killian stiffened.

"Looks like he's made his decision. It's the garage."

"Just like we figured. Good." Quin keyed the hand-held communicator beside him and spoke tersely. "The team is on it."

"They'd better be," Killian muttered, getting to his feet. He met Quin's eyes. "Don't miss."

Quin inclined his head as he picked up the case he had brought into the country when he had answered Killian's call. "You were the only target I ever missed."

Killian allowed himself one thin smile, although there was little humor in the gesture. "Just make sure you keep that record intact."

Silke was on edge. She could almost taste the danger in the air. For the first time since she had come to Atlanta she was without Killian at her side. She was cold and yet the sun was hot as she stepped from the building to the parking lot. It was only a short walk to the garage and her car, but she counted every step. Her instinct told her that the man sent to kill her was watching every move she made, just as he had watched her leave for work, alone, unescorted while Killian supposedly stayed home. The reality was that both he and Quin were close by. The trap had been set. The bait was tantalizingly unprotected. Patience was the name of the game and she hated it. Sighing deeply, carefully, so that she wouldn't arouse suspicion, Silke entered the garage. When a slender, pale man stepped out of the line of cars, she slowed. Nothing about him seemed to indicate a threat but somehow she knew. Maybe it was his eyes, the cold look that only one who understood pain and suffering would have worn. Her senses sharpened, but her step didn't falter as the distance between them lessened.

"No bodyguard this morning, Silke?" the man purred as he moved to block her way.

Silke stopped, her brows raised at a haughty angle. Killian had been very specific. His command: Stay in the open and give him, Quin, and the law enforcement team a chance to close in. "I don't know you," she murmured, buying time with conversation.

He smiled then.

Silke just barely controlled a shiver of revulsion. That was what death looked like, she decided.

"My name is Eric."

Silke started to take a step past him, playing his game. His hand wrapped around her arm, using exactly enough pressure to halt her forward momentum without causing pain. That would come later, when he could enjoy it to the last drop.

"You will come with me, please."

Silke shook her head, allowing just a little fear to creep into her behavior. Anger was really her most dominant emotion, anger that her life would be worth nothing more than a few dollars and that Killian, his friend, and the men who were even now listening in the shadows were also at risk. "No. My friend is waiting for me."

His smile flashed again as he shook his head. "No, I am." He reached for her handbag with his free hand, lifting it from her grasp despite her silent resistance and tossing it between the cars beside him. "And you won't need that." He urged her almost gently along in front of him toward a racy car backed into its slot.

Seeing it and knowing that, once she was inside, her odds of survival were instantly reduced, Silke felt the first real lick of fear. She couldn't see or feel Killian. Or Quin, Or the police. Her safety net was drawn carefully and precisely around the whole garage. Yet no one was making a move to help her. Logic and Killian's explanation ruled that they had to have an ironclad case of abduction for the courts. Any less and this killer and the man who hired him would be worked through the legal system on a lesser charge, a charge that very well might get both little more than judicial slaps on the wrist. But even as the thoughts formed, a demanding voice sounded in front of her and off to the right.

"Let her go!"

Killian swore furiously at the first word. He had told the chief he didn't want any damn hotheads or rookies on this job. He slipped from his hiding place, not one break in his almost silent string of oaths betraying the fear that snaked through him as he caught the flash of metal when Eric drew his gun.

"Dumb move, kid," Eric breathed, yanking Silke close as a shield, the muzzle of his gun tight against her heart. "Bet there are a bunch more of you fools in here," he added furiously, scanning the area. He prodded Silke hard with the weapon. "Tell them to show themselves and drop their guns. All of them, including your lover."

As though she could hear Killian's voice in her ear, Silke did just as he had instructed her this morning before she left.

If anything goes wrong, do exactly what he wants for as long as it takes to find your opening. I don't care what it takes, get out of there alive.

She moistened her lips. "He means it. Come out," she called. The fear that had begun to grow in her hardened; her survival instinct, honed over years and painful lessons, took over. Without moving, her body readied itself, her mind clearing of all thought but finding an opening, protecting herself, and, if possible, others. The game might have been instigated by a man she had never met and implemented by this one, but she no longer had to play by their rules.

Slowly, each man eased out of his hiding place. Eric didn't move or allow Silke to either.

"Where's your lover?" he hissed.

Silke thought fast. "He didn't figure you would be fool enough to try anything in here where you could be cornered. He's waiting outside." She put every ounce of quiver she could manage into her voice, letting her body go limp against him as much as she dared. She wanted to paint a picture of a woman becoming too frightened to cause trouble.

Eric's grip tightened on her arm as he tried to jerk her upright. Silke wasn't fast enough to stifle a groan of pain. Killian heard the small sound even as he closed the last few feet without detection. Rage billowed and was just as swiftly contained. Eric would pay for every bruise on Silke's body. But not until he had her safe.

"Hang on just a little longer, Silke," Killian murmured under his breath. All he needed was a clear shot. One single bead on Eric would do it. He dropped to one knee, steadied his hand, and homed in on his target. Outside, Quin would be getting impatient. It wouldn't be more than a few seconds before he would realize something had gone wrong and come hunting, slow, sure, and deadly. One more chance for Silke to survive.

Eric half carried Silke the last few feet toward his car. Killian tensed, cursing her courage and tactics even as he admired them. Eric was losing control of the situation. Suddenly one of the officers took a dive at his gun. Eric thrust Silke the car, shielding most of his body with hers as he snapped off a shot. Quin rushed the front entrance. Eric whirled. Killian rose from his crouch the second Eric's attention was diverted in the opposite direction, moving forward in a race for the gun that threatened Silke's life. Eric fired wildly, the gun bucking against Silke's side just before Killian hit the man, snatching Silke from his hands and thrusting himself in her place.

Silke had time for one scream of pain from the powder burn in her side before Killian's weight hit her, forcing her away from death, using his own body as a shield. She stumbled against the car beside her, nearly going down in the struggle, automatically reaching for the weapon Killian had given her. All around her, Silke caught glimpses of determined faces as those who had given up their weapons retrieved them. Suddenly, a shot rang out. Eric dropped to the concrete, clutching his chest while red bloomed around his fingers. Before Silke could do more than register the sudden silence, Killian was there, taking her in his arms, turning her head against his heart and from the man who would have killed her and enjoyed it.

"Don't look," he whispered against her hair as he walked her away from the place of violence to a shadowed corner.

Silke burrowed close to him in the half light. "Seems like the cavalry arrived in time," she murmured, wrapping her arms around him, feeling the race of his pulse beneath her cheek. Reaction was setting in, making her shiver.

"We try our poor best," he replied, running his hands over her back, feeling the tremors shaking her. His touch found the powder burns on her side. He leaned back, turning her a little without letting her go. His oath was savage as he surveyed the damage.

"It's not as bad as it looks," Silke said, stroking the hair back from his brow without even checking the injury. She just didn't care. She was alive. So was he. And so was his friend and the people who had tried to help them. That was more than enough.

"It looks like hell," he said succinctly.

She half smiled. "It burns like it, too."

Before he could say anything else, Quin walked up, carrying Silke's handbag. "You might want to put that gun away before you shoot Killian," he drawled, eyeing them both.

Silke blinked, then laughed unsteadily as she realized that although she hadn't had the gun Killian had given her pointed at his heart, it was definitely aimed in a direction guaranteed to hurt. Killian cursed again and plucked the small automatic out of her hands. He thrust it at Quin. "She doesn't need it anymore anyway." The rage seeped into his eyes as he looked over her head to the small group gathered around Eric.

"I didn't kill him."

"No, you damn well kept me from doing it," Killian replied, giving him a hard look.

Silke stared at both men. "What do you mean? I thought the idea was take him alive so he could testify against the supplier."

Killian said nothing, his body tense against hers.

Silke looked to Quin.

He handed her the purse, that not quite smile edging his lips. "Don't ask me. Ask him." He glanced over his shoulder. "But not here. Take her back to the apartment, Kill. I'll run interference for you."

"First I'm taking her to the hospital." Killian wrapped an arm around her shoulders and tucked her against his side.

"I don't want to go to the hosp . . ." She got nofarther. Killian's mouth stole the protest with one hard kiss.

They went to the hospital. And by the time the doctor had finished cleaning her injury, the police had caught up with them so there were questions to answer. When the call came in from Hollander to advise that the supplier had been arrested, all of them breathed a little easier. The timing had been one of the things that they had worked so hard to coordinate. Finally, the t's were crossed and the i's dotted so precisely that she, Killian, and Quin were allowed to leave. Silence ruled the drive back to the apartment. Silke had a number of questions, but having Quin as a voiceless onlooker wasn't conducive to probing. So she waited, tired physically with the demands that the danger had made on her body, but mentally and emotionally so wired that she wondered if she would ever come down.

All she could think about was the moment she had seen Eric train his sights on Killian, when Killian had thrust himself between her and death. One bullet could have taken his life, could have stolen from her a chance to reach for her own future without the fear born in the past. One small projectile could have stilled her heart, frozen her emotions in a limbo of dark gray without end. Emptiness. A world without Killian was truly empty. Alien. A stark landscape with no color, no light, no passion, no joy.

He had taught her trust. He had taught her desire. He had given her faith and his body and her own life. And love. She had given him her innocence that wasn't really innocence at all. She had given him lies. She had given him danger in her name. She had thought he had betrayed her. But now, with the memory of how easily her life could have been stripped of his presence, she faced the truth—that, had the situations been reversed, she would have made the same choices. If a lie would have saved him today, she would have gladly told any number of them. If her body between a gun and him would have given him one more moment on earth, she would have accepted that one bullet without regret.

Love. The word that had haunted her nightmares, terror of need and ownership, betrayal and greed. She had learned its worst imitators and closed her ears, heart, and eyes to its most truthful advocates. For years, she had given only a pale copy of love to her adoptive parents, holding herself aloof in ways that they must have known but hadn't been able to bridge. But no longer.

Killian had given her that gift, too. It was past time he knew it.

Killian walked Silke up the stairs, wondering what she was thinking. She had been so quiet on the drive home. He had put her reaction down to the stress of the day of waiting and the final confrontation. Now he wasn't so sure. There was a glow about her that said fatigue and the aftermath of an adrenaline high were the last things on her mind. He unlocked the door to her apartment, hoping as he hadn't hoped and prayed since he had seen that gun pressed against her heart. He shut out the world with the soft, closing snap of the door, then leaned against it, his arms folded across his chest.

"What is it?" he asked, his emotions too strung out to deal with the demands of finesse and subtlety.

Silke turned, her eyes searching his taut features, the glitter in his gaze that spoke of an equal mix of hope and determination. "I love you." She moved close until her body brushed his. Her look was bright with trust and faith, and all those emotions she had learned so long ago were just lies to trap the unwary. Killian had taught her those lies were only truths briefly disguised, that in his hands she would know only honesty. This man's honesty, given at cost to himself for her sake. "If you need forgiveness for the way we met, I give it. I saw Eric ready to shoot you and I knew that if one lie or a million would have stopped him I would have told it in an instant. More than that, I would have sold myself to him for your sake." She watched the knowledge of just how completely she had given herself to him sink in. She touched his suddenly pale skin, loving him as he was and as he would grow to be. He wasn't a perfect man, but for her he was the only man who could match her.

Killian closed his eyes, for one moment almost brought to his knees by the depth of her surrender. And yet it wasn't surrender, he realized a second later. It was a joining, a mating of her need for him to his for her. Was there any other on the face of the earth for whom he would give up his honor? He opened his eyes and still she was there. His woman. His Silke. He lifted his fingers, touching her lips, tracing their fullness.

"Say you'll marry me."

She didn't hesitate. Her smile was magic, pure Silke at her wicked best. "You name the day."

His smile was a match and checkmate to hers. "Tomorrow. I know people. Quin came in by his private jet. He can fly your people in for the ceremony. And be my best man. He even has an island that would make a perfect honeymoon spot."

She tipped back her head, laughter rippling softly through her. From the hell of tomorrows to the heaven of all the days to come like gold to spend freely lying in her hands. Here was the garden of Eden and Killian held the keys.

"I do like the way you plan. What if he doesn't go along with the idea?" she whispered, lifting her lips for his kiss.

He framed her face, his eyes glittering with a knowledge she didn't possess. He had a feeling that because of Silke, Quin just might have gotten something he had been seeking for a long time. Only time and patience would tell the tale. "He won't mind. He knows I'd do it for him," he murmured before accepting her invitation and extending one of his own.

Cool sheets, muted light, and the night to indulge their fantasies. Dreams, whispers in the darkness, and passion to set the mind on fire.

"Are you going to sleep away our wedding day?" Killian asked softly as he nuzzled Silke's neck, his lips tracing the length of her throat to first one breast, then the other.

She smiled drowsily, stretching and moving in an exquisite dance that was as old as man and woman and yet new again with Killian as her partner. "Are you trying to push me out of your bed already?" she asked, her mouth brushing his shoulders as she curved her body over him.

"Actually, it's your bed for the moment," he breathed against skin that still held the scent of his possession. He inhaled deeply, feeling primitive in a way that he knew he would always feel with Silke as his mate. "Your family will be here in less than an hour. You don't want them to find us here, do you?" He eased lower, reclaiming that which belonged, by her choice and his, to him.

Silke writhed as desire flashed, its claws unsheathing to capture. Her hands dug into his back as she arched to him. "I'll tell them you wouldn't let me up," she dared, her breath keeping time with the teasing forays of his tongue.

His laughter was a ripple of air over her sensitized flesh, another sensation to drive her ever closer to the edge of madness. Suddenly, her lashes lifted; for one crazy moment, reality intruded. "I don't have a thing to wear," she said in shock.

Killian rose above her, his body demanding a reward for its patience. He shifted into the cradle of her thighs, her heat a drug that he knew he'd never stopping craving. "Then wear me," he groaned, easing into her warmth.

Her eyes glittered, desire, humor, and love so potent a mix that she could have defied the gods of creation in that instant. "Gladly," she agreed huskily as she wrapped her arms around him to bind him safe in the wild ride to follow. Fulfillment came swiftly, hurried by need, by time racing through the hourglass of stolen moments. Then silence. Her soft laughter.

Killian raised his head, his brows quirked. "What is it?"

"When Mother asks what I plan to wear, I'm telling her I don't need a gown because I have you," she said, her eyes dancing with mischief.

"You do and I'll wring your neck," he promised, lifting himself off her and pulling her to her feet. He tapped her on the bottom. "Go start the shower while I make a call."

She propped her hands on her hips, giving him a look that women had been perfecting for centuries when men made the mistake of ordering instead of asking.

Killian wasn't dumb, and he was beginning to know his Silke. He kissed her quickly, molding her to him for one second. "It's a little surprise and I'm trying to make sure you don't hear me." He turned her toward the bathroom.

"I'm going. But this better not be one of those surprises that aren't all that nice."

"Would I do that?"

She glanced over her shoulder, her strength and pride undiminished by her nudity. "You might, if you thought you could get away with it."

He chuckled. "You know me."

She blew him a kiss. "Better every day."

Sun spilled into the room and the women gathered there. Silke sat amid the noise and confusion of her adoptive sisters and mother, thinking of the day in Lorraine's sitting room. Her mother had given her a new life, perhaps not in the way she had envisioned but no less wonderful. She smiled at her image and the reflection of Killian's surprise that hung on a padded hanger from the closet door. It was a dream of a wedding gown—sleek, wickedly sexy, and snow white. Virginal and vampish. Her smile widened at the words that had been scrawled in Killian's distinctive style on the card that had accompanied the dress. Quin had been the messenger. A different Quin, this time one who smiled just a little.

"Well, Silke, you beat us all," Caprice said softly, coming to stand beside Silke as she finished her makeup in front of the bathroom mirror.

"Do you think she had this in mind for us?"

Caprice shrugged, glancing back to their mother, who was still murmuring over the dress that man had brought. "I wouldn't put it past her."

Silke laughed, her eyes clear of every doubt, every nightmare. "Then I hope all of you have the same luck I have."

Caprice shook her head even as she hugged Silke close. "Somehow I think the rest of us will have a bit more trouble with our rites of passage than you did."

Silke turned, meeting her sister's eyes, thinking of all of the things that Caprice didn't know, the things she probably would never know about her own rite of passage. "Try having a little faith, Caprice."

Lorraine eased into the bathroom. "Darling, couldn't you have found time to at least get a chair for the apartment?" she teased.

Silke hugged the mother of her heart. "Not on the money you sent me here with. I used up almost all of my capital getting a roof over my head and food in the fridge as it was."

Lorraine frowned. "But your father and I were sure we had enclosed enough." She looked to Caprice. "Is your place like this?"

Caprice shook her head. "No, much worse."

Lorraine's frown deepened. "I must talk to your father. He won't like this at all." She started to leave, then remembered why she had interrupted. "Oh, darling, Quin said the limo is ready whenever you are."

Noelle joined them, bringing the dress and Leora to help. "You aren't getting nervous are you?" she asked, for once not vague at all.

Silke smiled, her expression serene as it had never been. "Not about Killian. Never." She took her gown, his surprise. "Let's get this marriage on the road. My man is waiting."

"Do you know I believe this is the first wedding I have ever attended, much less helped implement," Quin murmured as he and Killian stood at the altar, waiting for the music of the bridal procession to begin. There were few guests, but those who were there mattered to Killian and Silke.

Killian glanced at Quin. "You did a good job even if you didn't manage to pull it together in a day. I wasn't sure even you could command a church on less than a month's notice."

Quin's lips quirked. "The church was relatively easy. Getting that gown was tough. I still don't know why you didn't just let Silke get one herself instead of making sure she was too busy to think of it."

"She doesn't see herself as I do. We would have fought over what it looked like and I was determined to have my way."

Quin's brows rose. "What if she hated it?"

"She wouldn't. I know my Silke." Killian grinned, just as the organist struck the first note. "Besides, I'd have taken her wrapped in a bed sheet if that's the only way I could have her." He turned, looking toward the back of the church, waiting as it seemed he had been waiting since that first night.

Then she was there, framed in the doorway. His breath caught. Her beauty was a bright banner that streaked through his senses, leaving a trail of fire in its wake. His Silke. The dress was all he had hoped it would be. It whispered of the innocence that he had shared and that she didn't believe was hers. It murmured of her passion, her flame of life. It embraced her body as his arms would always hold her close. But most of all, it was his tribute, his idea of his Silke. He smiled faintly, triumph in his eyes as she drew near. Pride muted the triumph and awe spiced the whole.

Silke read the look in his eyes, never having felt more a woman than she did at this moment. Her hand slipped into his. She needed no one to give her to this man, although her father would have gladly walked these last feet with her. Instead, she came alone, watched by those who loved her. She wore no veil. She no longer needed to hide what she thought and felt. She belonged to Killian. His choice and hers.

Killian lifted her hand to his lips, holding her eyes. "I love you."

Her fingers brushed his lips, her smile touching him with its radiant confidence in him, herself, and the future they would make. "As I love you. For now. For always."

As if that were an agreed upon signal, they turned as one to face the man who would read words that they didn't really need, who would proclaim to the world what they already knew. They were married, heart, soul, and body. One.

COMING NEXT MONTH

#9 ALL ABOUT EVE *by Patty Copeland*
Eve Sutton was just an hour away from her destination when her car sputtered to a halt. And a stranded tourist was the very last thing Dr. Adam Wagner needed.

#10 THE CANDY DAD *by Pat Pritchard*
A down-to-earth single suburban mom was hardly his type but Jesse Daniels couldn't deny the sweet fantasies Rennie Sawyer inspired.

#11 BROKEN VOWS *by Stephanie Daniels*
When Wendy Valdez' smile melted his heart, Jack O'Connor didn't know how to respond. It would be easy to fall—fast and hard—for this tempting woman.

#12 SILENT SONG *by Leslie Knowles*
Nicole Michael couldn't believe it was him. Had Jake Cameron discovered the reason she'd left him so abruptly?

Plus four other great romances!

AVAILABLE THIS MONTH:

#1 PERFECT MATCH
Pamela Toth

#2 KONA BREEZE
Darcy Rice

#3 ROSE AMONG THORNES
Pamela Macaluso

#4 CITY GIRL
Mary Lynn Dille

#5 SILKE
Lacey Dancer

#6 VETERAN'S DAY
GeorgeAnn Jansson

#7 EVERYTHING ABOUT HIM
Patricia Lynn

#8 A HIGHER POWER
Teresa Francis